*For Brian —
with best wishes —
[signature] 10/20/99*

NO PETS

Jim Ray Daniels

Working Lives Series
Bottom Dog Press
Huron, Ohio

© Copyright 1999
Jim Ray Daniels & Bottom Dog Press
Huron, Ohio 44839
ISBN 0-933087-54-3 $10.95
Ph. 419-433-5560

Cover Art:
Bacon, Francis. *Dog.* (1952) Oil on canvas
The Museum of Modern Art, NY.
William A. M. Durden Fund.
Photograph © 1999 The Museum of Modern Art
Cover Design:
Frank Lehner
Layout Design:
Larry Smith

Acknowledgments:

We thank the following publications where these stories first appeared:

Michigan Quarterly Review: "Wrestling"
Witness: "Black Box"
Getting By: Stories of Working Lives: "All Packed"
Arete: The Journal of Sport Literature: "Shooting a Few"
The Bridge: "Seeds"
The MacGuffin: "Tunnel to Canada"
Bellingham Review: "Night Shopping"
The Long Story: "No Pets"
"No Pets" was turned into a screenplay by the author, and *No Pets*, an independent feature film directed by Tony Buba, was released in 1994 by Braddock Films.

Ohio Arts Council
A STATE AGENCY
THAT SUPPORTS PUBLIC
PROGRAMS IN THE ARTS

Table of Contents

Movie Stars
7

Wrestling
19

Black Box
35

All Packed
51

Tunnel to Canada
65

Shooting a Few
79

Seeds
87

Night Shopping
97

No Pets
107

Movie Stars

"Get your coat on," my mother said. "We'll miss our bus."

My brothers and sisters were at school, so my mother and I were alone in the silent house. It suddenly seemed huge, and I lingered in my room, lazily swaying between the two empty bunk beds where all the boys slept.

She stood in the doorway smiling. "Does somebody want to stop at the Coney Island for lunch?" she asked. I grinned.

I'd worn glasses from the age of three. I scratched the lenses on cement, I broke off temple pieces, I took them off and forgot them in strange places. Once they were missing for a week until turning up in a neighbor's milk chute. I had carefully placed them there while we had a Free-for-All. Most of our games involved trying to inflict bodily harm on each other. One time both temple pieces were torn off during a game of Kill-the-Guy-with-the-Ball. I was used to seeing wads of white tape in my peripheral vision. I was the only kid in the family who wore them. Me and my mother.

My parents were still married, though later they'd both say it was only for our sake. The house was small, so they had to sleep together in the same bed. They couldn't avoid touching each other, I guess, because they kept having children in between battles. They could never decide how old we'd have to be before it'd be okay to split up. Finally, after we'd all moved out, they quickly got divorced.

My brothers and I would lay awake on our bunks in silence, listening while they fought. I kept my eyes open, believing this would make it end sooner. All I could see above me was the faint outline of the bed boards beneath the top bunk where my oldest brother Steve lay. My glasses sat folded on the dresser. I could reach out and touch them to make sure they were there, and sometimes I did.

Occasionally, after a particularly long, ugly fight, my father disappeared. Once I heard my mother whispering loudly on the phone: "Get back here, you coward." I hated when she cried. I ran outside and cried myself. My father always returned. He never packed anything when he left. He'd just storm out. We'd hear the door slam, the car start, and my mother's fists pounding something. Some days, I still hear my mother's loud whisper in the wind: "Get back here."

"We won't be late, mom," I said. Ten years old, I was trying to take better care of my glasses. Suddenly I was combing my hair on a regular basis, though I couldn't say why. I grabbed my winter coat, and we hurried out to stand alone at the cold corner and wait. I danced on the curb, craning my neck to spot our bus down the long straight line of Eight Mile Road. My mother was counting change. I was counting my good luck to have bad eyes and my mother all to myself.

We had to change buses at the fairgrounds. My job was to hold our transfers. I loved the idea of getting another ticket, getting on another bus, continuing the journey. "Could we get transfers and go all the way to Florida?" I asked as we climbed aboard. We'd never been to Florida, never would go—that heaven we dreamed of during our long, gray winters.

The bus driver snorted, "You can get as far as River Rouge, but there ain't no beaches in River Rouge. Just snow, same as here."

"We'll be lucky if we ever get as far as Ohio," my mother said, and we stepped to the back of the bus, sitting next to each other in the middle of the last row where the seat went all the way across. Anyone getting on would be walking down the aisle toward my mother, the queen of the bus. She wore make-up and perfume to go to town, and to me she looked glamorous. She was dyeing her hair blond, even back then, and it was poofed up with hair spray.

My father worked for Chrysler's, like most everybody in our neighborhood. He smoked Lucky's non-filtered till they seemed to disappear into his lips. My mother smoked True Blue. True Green was the menthol brand. My mother liked to say "True Blue," winking when she said it.

I watched the buildings grow taller, the streets cleaner. I squirmed and twisted on the vinyl seat, and so did my mother. We only had one car, so my mother was usually stuck with us at home. I could tell she loved these bus trips too. Downtown was a world of magic entrances—revolving doors, escalators, elevators. The smell hit me as soon as I stepped off the bus: possibility.

My mother was getting her eyes checked too. She wore cat-eye frames which my father hated. "Meow," she said to that. After all six kids were in school, she took a job at the Knights of Columbus Credit Union down the street. My father was a member because their bar served cheap drinks, and they had a good bowling league. What made it good, I don't know, but that's what he told us. This all probably makes my dad sound like a lunkhead. Some of the time he was, but he was a thinker too. That was his problem—thinking made him unhappy. Or not having enough time to think. His big hobby was the weather, and he had ambitions of being a TV weatherman. The most popular local weatherman, Sunny Day, drove him absolutely nuts. "I bet Sunny's not even his real name," he'd say, as if that were some great insight.

Sunny had this shtick—he'd say, "tomorrow there'll be clouds and rain, so it's going to be clainy" and he'd write "clainy" on his map of Michigan. Part of the Upper

Peninsula detached from the map, and he used to take it off and wave it around. A real riot.

Dr. Keith's office was in one of the old skyscrapers downtown where everything shone and smelled like polish. I felt like I was entering the church of some other religion, a better one, when we walked into the huge lobby. My mother held my hand when we got on the elevator—something we never ever did at home, where she didn't have enough hands for all of us. She was a different person on those trips. If my father'd had bad eyes, they might have been happier.

We had little family in Detroit. My father was an only child, and both his parents had died in a car accident shortly after his marriage. My mother had family, but it was back in Arkansas. She'd met my father when he was stationed there in the army. Our neighbors were busy raising their own kids, who were all around our ages, so there were no babysitters to be had. My father worked a lot of overtime during those years anyway. The point is, they never went anywhere without us.

In the doctor's office, I quickly scanned the kids' magazines because once we got our drops, they'd simply be taunting me. The drops did something to our eyes which made everything blurry. Their only plus was that afterwards we got to wear these cheap plastic dark glasses, and we could pretend to be movie stars. I was always Jackie Gleason, and my mother was always Lucy, Lucille Ball.

"And away we go!" I'd say. I picked Jackie Gleason because he was so fat, he seemed like the biggest star, and he had my name and I was a bit of a butterball myself. My father loved Jackie, who was on TV every Saturday night, the one night we spent together as a family. Bath night, and we always fought to get our baths in before Jackie came on. I felt clean just thinking about it—clean and happy piled on the couch with everyone I loved, nobody fighting, everybody laughing, even when we didn't get the jokes.

"Oh, Ricky," my Mom would say to any little thing I did. Or "Wa-wa-wa!" She and my father never fought the way Ricki and Lucy fought on TV—half-joking, ready to make up. With my parents, the stakes were always higher. Their fights lasted a long time, even if they were over grocery money or a stain on the carpet, a lawn full of weeds or a broken window and who was going to fix it, who was going to pay?

The doctor was amazed: the muscle weakness which made me cross-eyed was continuing to correct itself. If it kept improving, I wouldn't need glasses anymore. I didn't share his enthusiasm. Without glasses, I'd be just like the other kids. I sulked alone in the waiting room while my mother got examined. It'd be hours before the drops wore off. At the Coney Island down the block where we always ate after our check-ups, we'd sit at the counter by the bathrooms where we could watch everybody while we ate. I'd eat two dogs with everything—cheese, onions, chili. French fries. Large root beer. I didn't know if my mother had enough money, but if this was going to be one of our last trips downtown together, I wanted to make sure it was memorable.

My mother emerged, beaming in her movie star glasses. "Cha-cha-cha," she cried, jumping up and down. My mother would do anything on those trips. An old man reading *Time* looked up, startled, then frowned. She ignored him. "Isn't it wonderful, sweetie, you might not have to wear glasses anymore! And you look so handsome without your glasses—the girls will be crawling all over you!" She took me in her arms. The top of my head reached her shoulder, which put my face uncomfortably close to her breasts. I pulled away.

"I don't *want* girls crawling all over me," I said.

"Just wait and see." Putting on her coat, she knocked her dark glasses off. The shock of seeing her naked eyes frightened me, and I quickly picked up the glasses and handed them to her. Mine fell off while I was bending down, and she started laughing hysterically. "The blind leading the blind," she said, "now, where's our Seeing Eye dog?" She started groping around. "Is that you, sweetie?" she said to the coat tree, "my, how you've grown." I started laughing too. My mother's laugh was dangerously contagious. It often got her in trouble at home, my father asking, "What's so funny?" He was usually immune to it, though it seemed to infect everybody else. Even the old man was smiling now as we careened out the door and down the hall toward the elevator.

I was laughing, but I felt a cold burn inside—I was hungry, but it was more than that. No more trips downtown, girls crawling all over me—what next? Back through the revolving door and onto the street, my mother hurried, looking at her watch. She suddenly stopped in the middle of the wide sidewalk and turned to me.

"Jackie," she said, streaming words together like she did when she was nervous. "You remember Mr. Coggins' brother, the man who lived next door when the Togginses went away last year? You know, you're going to be such a handsome young man—I should start calling you Jack, you know that? Anyway, Jack—Bill, Mr. Coggins' brother, he teaches here in town and I think he's going to meet us for lunch!" She seemed much too cheery, as if she was trying to will her excitement on to me.

She quickly grabbed my arm and started walking again, touching her hair as if to adjust something, though the spray held each hair rigidly in place. She had said what she needed to say and did not want a response.

"You *think* he's going to meet us?" was all I could think to say as she yanked me along. We never ate out as a family. I mean *never*. "Take six kids to a restaurant, are you kidding?" my father'd say, reaching back to pat his wallet to make sure it was still there.

"I told him we'd be there, and he said he'd try to meet us, now let's hurry."

"We don't need nobody having lunch with us." I didn't like Bill Coggins. He'd told me to call him Bill when he lived next door, and I never called any grown-ups by their first name. He was that kind of guy—someone I'd later call a "smoothie" once I learned the word. His older brother'd gotten a temporary assignment in California for six months and took his family with him. Bill, younger, single, moved in to keep an eye on things—and enjoy the free rent.

The Cogginses never quite fit into our neighborhood. Mr. Coggins was an engineer at the GM Tech Center, a step above the factory workers who lined our streets. We had Mr. Adam, who owned two barber shops and lived in the big house on the corner, but he was a "card"—another word I'd learn soon—and kept everybody laughing, so no one begrudged him what he had.

The Cogginses kept to themselves. When they went away, it took awhile for anyone to even notice. But then the young, handsome stranger was spotted, and that gave everyone something to talk about, particularly after my mother was seen leaning over the fence into their yard and laughing that laugh on a regular basis while my father was away at work. Bill Coggins was a schoolteacher out for the summer, so he had time on his hands. When my mother noticed him in his yard, she'd go to the bathroom to spruce up, then step outside to check her flower garden.

That's what was next—we were having lunch with Bill Coggins. I wasn't going to call him Bill, I knew that much.

We sat at a booth instead of the counter, so there'd be room for him. She let me order, but she herself just had coffee, hoping, I guess, to eat with Bill Coggins. I had to strain my neck to see as my mother pointed out a ridiculous hat, a pretty dress, a bad toupee. She was charged up, even before her second cup. The Cogginses had been back from California for six months. I hadn't known my mother'd even spoken to Bill once he moved out.

While we waited, I read her facts about U.S. presidents printed on the sugar packets. She nodded distractedly, her eyes trained on the doorway. "What's a Whig?" I asked. "What's a Whig?"

"I don't know, dear," she replied, "I don't know."

"Do you think Dad knows?" I asked.

She closed her eyes and sighed, but she didn't answer.

I quickly went to work on my two hot dogs when they arrived. "Jackie, you're making a mess," she said, though usually she didn't care. I could feel chili dripping over my chin. I swiped at my face with a napkin and took another huge bite.

"What's your hurry?...Give me a bite, will you?" I reluctantly handed her the last dog, and she ripped it in half. She had taken off her dark glasses, even though we weren't supposed to, not yet.

"He teaches chemistry," she said. "He's a scientist."

"He ain't coming," I said hopefully. I slurped my root beer, sucking the last sips from between the ice cubes. The waitress suddenly appeared. "Will there be anything else?" she asked, our check in her hand. At the counter, they never bothered us. I wanted to spin around like we did on the stools—both of us laughing, not caring. Wedged between the bench and the table, I felt like we were already on the bus headed home. I sat up on my feet and looked around— the restaurant had filled with businessmen in suits.

"Yes, yes there will," my mother said, and she ordered two hot dogs for herself. "You want another one?" she asked, pulling me back into my seat. I nodded eagerly. "Another root beer too?"

"Yeah, a float," I said, "a root beer float, please." I knew I had her at a disadvantage. She frowned, but the waitress was already gone, my dirty plate shedding used napkins behind her. I took off my dark glasses too.

"Oh well," she said, her voice cracking slightly. We waited in silence now, as if she really was blind to everything around us. Her hands nervously pulled at the large gold buttons of her dress like she was trying to squeeze them smaller. She tore into her hot dogs when they came. The chili stained the corners of her mouth. I had never eaten three before. I had never even dreamed of three. I found the room for another, and forced down the last bite.

My mother ate them so fast, she had to order herself dessert to kill more time. The waitress just wanted us to leave, though the lunch crowd was beginning to thin out. I was stuffing my pockets with sugar packets.

"He must've gotten busy and couldn't get away," she said.

"He wanted me to call him Bill," I said, as if that explained everything. Even back then, I knew schoolteachers had a set lunch hour.

My mother looked at her watch again. She never wore a watch at home. "Shit," she said—which she never said. Only when something precious broke, and we had few precious things. "We've got to run."

"I gotta use the bathroom," I said suddenly. I was ready to explode.

"Well, hurry up then," she snapped, and started counting out the money for the bill. When I came out, she was standing at the counter by the door waiting for me. My stomach was cramped, so I took slow, careful steps.

"You're going to make us late," she said, "Let's go." As we got to the door, the waitress ran up, "Something wrong with the service?" she spat out.

My mother had left no tip. "I—I'm sorry. I just have enough for bus fare home. I thought I had more. I'm sorry."

"Get outta here," the waitress said, pointing as if we didn't know the way.

I thought my mother might cry, but she just stumbled out onto the sidewalk in a daze. She ran ahead to the bus stop, leaving me to follow. A bus was pulling away, probably ours.

"Don't tell your father about this," she pleaded angrily as we stood waiting forever for the next bus. She didn't mean the expensive lunch. She didn't mean being late. It began to rain, and we had no umbrella. My father had predicted rain, but he usually did. While he was inside the dark factory all day, he didn't want anybody else having any sunshine.

The bus ride home seemed incredibly slow, my mother sighing in irritation at every slow person getting off or on. I looked over at her watch—my brothers and sisters were on their way home from school with no one at home to meet them. When we finally got to our stop, my mother yanked me down the steps.

From the corner, I could see the others sitting on the porch or playing in the snow. My youngest sister Abbey was crying. Andy and Eric were spinning around a telephone pole. The others were having a Free-for-All on the lawn with some of the neighborhood kids. Mrs. Hunter from across the street was talking to my brother Steve. He spotted us and pointed. My mother began wildly sprinting up the street, holding the house key tight in her fist. I ran behind her yelling, "Hey, hey!" She held her arms high above her, reaching up as if something was trying to pull her under. "We missed our bus," she was shouting, almost gasping. It was close enough to the truth, and I wasn't telling. Movie stars have all kinds of secrets. I tossed my glasses on top of a snow bank, then I ran up and leaped onto the pile of bodies wrestling in the snow.

Wrestling

When the Big O and I fought, nobody got hurt. We'd wrestle and curse each other. If one of us got the advantage, it meant the Hindu Torture. The Hindu involved sticking a blade of grass up the other person's nose. I have no idea where we got this from. If anyone knows, give me a call. Tickles like hell. That's how our fights ended—in laughter.

The Big O was my best friend, Phil. Big as in fat, O as in O'Malley. He liked having that nickname. He didn't have much else distinguishing about him except having bigger breasts than any guy I knew, which made gym class pretty rough for him.

O was a year ahead of me in school. When he was in the 10th grade and I was in 9th, we had Electronics together with Mr. North. Mr. North said things like "No matter how much you shake and dance, a few drops always ends up in your pants."

"He should be teaching poetry with shit like that," O used to say. The O was my electronics partner, and together we were making a battery charger for when he got a car. We'd make sure that car's battery would never run down. Driving to school was our ultimate dream—we fantasized about driving to Belly Buster's for lunch. We'd walked to and from school together since forever it seemed, carrying our stupid brown bags.

Fatass Andrews and Ed Greelish, two rockers, also walked to school together. I never knew Fatass's real first name. Even Mr. North called him Fatass. He dwarfed the

Big O. He'd flunked at least once, just like Ed G. We called them the Tag-team Flunkies, though our own grades were nothing to brag about. Edgy was one of the mute rockers, and Fatass one of the mouthy ones, so they made a balanced team. They both lived over on Dallas, two streets away from ours, on the other side of Ryan Road, the main drag. Dallas, the street of tough guys. I don't know what they did different over there, but they had more rockers per square inch than any street I know—Terry Rucker Mother Fucker, the three Rotelli brothers, Bill Earl and his cousin Tom who moved from Lincoln High because they didn't have a street tough enough for him over there. And that's just the first few houses.

I think Ed G. lifted weights or something. He wasn't big—just strong. He wore tight, short-sleeve shirts that bulged his muscles. He and Fatass always wore black shirts and jeans, and big shit-kicker boots, even in summer when you know their feet must've been sweating like pigs in there. I never understood how rockers could wear long black jeans all summer long and never sweat. I guess that's why I'd never make a good rocker. I have never in my entire life seen a rocker's legs outside of gym class. Even in gym class, you could still tell the rockers because they wore black socks.

It's not like O and I were wimps or anything. We both smoked, and I believe we'd won the under-sixteen tag-team shoplifting crown the previous year, though Steve Monchak and Paul Lipton might have won if Paul hadn't gotten caught stealing cigars at Charlie's Market and been grounded for two months. Besides, we were in the dummy classes. Only the brainy guys could be real wimps. If you were a wimp *and* a dummy, the rockers pretty much left you alone.

We shoplifted at Bur-Ler's, our local variety store. Sandra, our friend who worked there, looked the other way when we slid out with jeans and records tucked under our bulky winter coats. Summer was a problem—we just took candy and little shit then. Lots of kids got their first jobs there. They paid less than minimum wage. Bur—Mr. Burman—didn't care what anybody thought. The kids needed the money, so they didn't squawk. For the O and I, shoplifting was our kind of squawking—squawking on the sly.

The thing about Fatass was that he had a tough-guy reputation, but he could rarely catch anybody, so his threats had a limit. Like a rhino, he was only good for one quick burst. He might have made a good heavyweight wrestler, if he'd been willing to cut his hair and play by the rules—the limits of the mat would've been a big help to him.

After I pinned Edgy in the gym class wrestling tournament—not only pinned him, but did it in fifteen seconds—the real trouble started. He was strong, but I knew the holds. When the O and I were in junior high, we used to go to the high school wrestling matches because they only cost thirty-five cents, while the basketball games cost a buck. And we liked to go see big Bill Chatka wrestle. He was the heavyweight king. When Chatka took somebody down, the gym floor shook. We ate our Bur-Ler's candy and sat in the front row chanting "Chatka, Chatka, Chatka," till he pinned the poor guy. Chatka had pretty big boobs too, but nobody said shit to him. The Big O cried when he lost in the state finals to this guy who looked more like a sumo wrestler—so big he made even Chatka look small.

I knew the holds because O and I used to practice on each other on my front lawn. The sidewalk and driveways marked the edges of our mat. We'd lose ourselves to the careful, intimate holds, giving each other points for take downs, escapes, riding time, our bodies close, warm, sweaty with change.

I'd gotten Edgy in a cross-face cradle before he knew what hit him. *Bam*, down came Coach Zeus's hand: Pin. Maybe I overdid the celebrating a little—O and I gave each other high fives, and I stomped around the mat like Bobo Brazil from "Big-Time Wrestling" on TV. Edgy sat up on the mat and glowered. As usual, he didn't say a word, though he looked more menacing on his knees than standing erect. All the other rockers in class were laughing.

Fatass didn't have to take gym class—it was a great mystery why. "If we could only find out how he got out of gym, he'd be eating out of our hands, I just know it," O said on more than one occasion. The O suspected Fatass had bigger boobs than he did. Fatass certainly didn't wear tight t-shirts like Edgy—his shirts were more like huge black tents flapping in the breeze, a couple of stakes pulled loose. I think he got out of gym simply because he was too fat.

The O hated Fatass with a passion ever since he had succeeded in getting a hold of the O in the school parking lot one morning before school—snuck up from behind and got him in a headlock. At the time, he wasn't particularly pissed off at O, but being a rocker, he wanted to rough somebody up, just on principle—keep the rep up, you know—and O was an easy target. He started walking around holding O in the headlock. "Let's go for a walk, O'Malley," he said. I was standing there with a bunch of other guys waiting for the bell. Fatass seemed like he was joking, so I didn't worry too much. Then he pushed O's head down by his crotch and said, "C'mon homo, suck my dick."

O was pleading, "C'mon, let me go, Fatass, c'mon." Fatass was clearly enjoying the attention of his captive audience. "Oh Philip," he said, "that feels so good. Suck me like a good homo." O was starting to cry, I could tell. I didn't know if the others could tell yet or not, but I knew how his voice cracked when he started to lose it. The last thing you ever wanted to do was cry in front of a bunch of guys. It'd be all over then. The only one who could get away with that was the pro wrestler, Crybaby McCarthy, and that's because everyone knew the crying was fake.

"What'd you call me?"

The O must've been confused. Fatass let everybody call him that, and suddenly he was taking offense. "What'd you call me?"

O mumbled, "Fatass." He was choking back tears—his face was crumbling, right up there beneath Fatass's big belly. The bell rang just then, though Fatass wasn't one to pay a lot of attention to bells. He was in no hurry to graduate, especially when he could pick on guys like O for years to come.

"It's *Mister* Fatass to you. Call me Mister Fatass." His first name must have been something really goofy like Francis.

"Mr. Fatass," Phil said, so quiet we could barely hear him. Most of the other guys were laughing. Some just shook their heads and headed into school. A few stuck around, hoping yet to see some blood.

"Louder."

"Mr. Fatass!" Since most of the crowd was in the school now, he let O go. Phil ran away, and I ran after him. I caught him easily, out by the football field. He was whoofing and wheezing, "Mother fucker, goddamn mother fucker," really crying now, letting it out. I handed him the handkerchief I carried for my allergies—didn't want to be slinging snot all over the school. He blew his nose and looked at me, quiet now. A look that said "I can't help it if I'm a wimp."

"No shame in it," I lied. O tried to hand me my handkerchief back. "Keep it," I said, "I got a million of them."

What Fatass did to him was worse than getting your ass kicked. "Everybody knows you're no homo," I said. He bit his lip and wiped his nose again.

"Damn straight," he said finally.

"I mean, who can take Fatass?" I said quickly. "Nobody in the tenth grade—at least once he gets a hold of you."

"Maybe Tommy Conway. I think he could take him," O said, serious now, happy to be talking away from himself.

"Yeah, maybe Conway. Conway, and maybe 'The Brute.'"

"Brute Bennett? No, no way."

"I don't think Fatass even got a dick," I said. "That's why he don't have to take gym. Guy ain't got no dick." In our high school, the boys swam naked. We both got a good laugh out to clear the air. O laughed long and hard, extending the laugh till it was just him, forcing it. "We're late for school, buddy," he said suddenly.

"No shit," I said, and together we headed back.

After that, Fatass used to yell at us across Ryan Road when we walked home from school, him and Edgy on one side, us on the other. Four lanes of heavy traffic between us—no way Fatass was going to get across without getting bounced in the air like a giant beach ball. "Phil-up, ya gonna come over and suck my dick again? C'mon Philip, you fucking homo." And to me, "Hey Buford, you big shissshy, why don't you shay shomeshing." I'd just about overcome my speech defect, but Fatass had a long memory, and he went with what he had. He didn't have much imagination when it came to talking trash. We just ignored him, mumbling and stumbling home on our side of Ryan.

The day I pinned Edgy, I met O after school by the 10th grade lockers, like usual. Fatass had been telling everybody that Edgy was going to get me on the way home. Ed G. could run and maybe catch me if it came down to it. Running from Fatass was a game, except for someone like the O. Fatass was such a freak, no one would call you a coward for running away. You could laugh about it later— "Yeah, got away from Fatass today. Close call. Ha, ha, ha." But Edgy, he was in my wrestling weight class, and hadn't I just pinned his sorry ass with my cross-face cradle? Why should I be afraid to take him on?

I had this problem with fighting: I didn't like getting punched. It hurt. Wrestling was fine, but nobody wrestled anymore, not out on the street where it counted. Street fighting with a rocker—well, they didn't call them shit-kicker boots for nothing. O walked up with a book in his hand.

"Whoa, what's with the book?" I asked, trying to keep things light. It was a matter of pride in our school not to be seen lugging books home, especially if you were tracked dumb like O and me. Those biology guys could take books home, but not us Future Shoprats of America. Hell, you could get kicked out of the club for that. We couldn't imagine ourselves working in a factory, but we weren't able to imagine anything else either. Nothing that paid a decent wage.

"Some English I gotta read," he said sheepishly. "Oral report."

"Oral report. Bummer." With my speech defect, I dreaded any occasion that required public speaking.

"Yeah," he said. "I'd better load up on the deodorant tomorrow." He lifted his arms, and I saw the huge dark stains. I looked down at the book. *Animal Farm,* by George Orwell. "A farm book?"

"Never mind," he said. "You'll have to read it next year."

"Listen," I said, "we gotta ditch Fatass and Edgy — Fatass said Edgy's gonna kick my ass."

"Oh, man, I knew something like this was gonna happen. Why'd you have to go and pin him?"

"I couldn't help it. The ghost of Chatka took over." Chatka, our hero, had been shot and killed in an armed robbery the year after he graduated. He was working at a party store when these two guys came in with guns. Chatka against one guy with a gun, I'd take Chatka. Two guys? He didn't have a chance. Only on "Big-Time Wrestling" did one guy ever take two.

We snuck out the side of the school opposite from where we lived and headed over to Bur-Ler's.

"Sandy says they got some new albums in," I said.

"We can't steal no albums. We ain't got jackets."

"Oh, yeah. Well, let's check 'em out for the next cool day." It was mid-May, warm enough for short sleeves. For big sweat stains. Ass-kicking weather.

Sandy was just putting on her Bur-Ler's smock when we walked in.

"Hey Sandy," I said.

"Hey Timmy," she said. Sandy was the only one who still called me Timmy besides my mother. I let her because we'd been babies together—she lived right next door and was the closest thing to a sister I was ever going to get.

"Hey Sandy," O said.

"Oh, it's the little one," she said. The Big O winced. That went back to last summer when we were sleeping in the tent in my yard and Sandy snuck out of her house and came over and we played strip poker. It was something O and I had done together ourselves once—then we'd run around the block naked, the cool, crazy wind blowing over our pale skin and mad laughter.

Sandy added a new exciting element. We didn't kiss—we were too close for that—but I got a hard-on for her. The O stayed soft, and he covered up fast. I thought it was mean of Sandy to bring that up, but sometimes she seemed jealous of the O and me.

O made a face at her. I could see him trying to think of a clever reply, then giving up. We checked out the new albums, hiding the ones to steal in the back of the stacks so people who were actually looking to buy couldn't find them. After that, we wandered around the store killing time, but Mr. "Ler" Lerman followed us, finally asking, "Can I help you boys?" in a way that pointed to the door. We headed out, thinking maybe it was safe, but rounding the corner to the Rat Place, the empty lot between Bur-Ler's and A&P, we bumped right into Fatass and Edgy.

"Shit," I mumbled, backing up a step. Bad things always happened in the Rat Place. Some kind of curse kept it vacant—rutted in winter, weedy in summer. Trashy always. Nothing would ever be built there. It was where the development of our neighborhood had crested before it began to recede into unemployment and boarded-up storefronts.

"Hey boys," Fatass said with a big evil smile on his face. He had this voice, kind of lispy and threatening at the same time—gave me the creeps.

"Edgy here has a score to settle." I think Fatass watched too many gangster movies.

"Buford don't want to fight," O said. If he knew one thing about me, he knew I didn't want to fight.

"Stay out of this, little one," Fatass said. O and I quickly looked at each other, wondering, *Sandy*? It quickly silenced Phil.

Edgy looked at Fatass, who nodded, "Go get him, Ed." He was like the Weasel, the Sheik's manager on "Big-Time Wrestling." Sheik never said a word because he supposedly didn't speak English. The Weasel did all the talking. I'm sure Edgy knew a few words like "Duh" and "Fuck you." Edgy rushed up and started choking me. I grabbed his arms and twisted, and we both fell on the dirt and gravel. No grass, so the Hindu was definitely not an option.

We were rolling on the edge of the Rat Place, spilling back over into the parking lot, and he kept trying to punch me, but I was squirming and twisting so he couldn't get any leverage. Edgy was breathing hard and saying "punk" over and over. Fatass was yelling "Punch him, Ed, kick his fucking ass." The O was dancing around, trying to stay outside the limits of a Fatass charge. Some of the other Dallas rockers wandered over from Kowalski's Drugs, where they bought their cigarettes. A large circle of bodies swirled around me.

"Get 'em, Buford," somebody yelled. I was so surprised to hear my own last name that I almost took a punch from Edgy flush on the jaw. I twisted, and he hit the top of my head, hurting his knuckles. That just made him more pissed off. He was on top of me, and I couldn't seem to shake him. He was getting in a few good licks, and it was starting to sink in that I was in the process of getting my ass kicked.

Then out of nowhere an enormous rocker I'd never seen before lifted Edgy off me in one smooth motion. He looked at me, "Are you a Buford? Larry's brother?"

"Yeah," I said, spitting dust and trying not to cry.

"Do you want to fight this guy?"

"No, not really," I said, as if I was thinking it over.

He grabbed Edgy and kicked him in the ass with one of the pointiest, shiniest, slickest shit-kickers I've ever seen. They made Fatass's look like those flimsy rubber boots we used to wear in winter. He wheeled around, "What are you looking at, Fatass?" I bet he didn't even know that was his nickname. I bet he was just calling him that. "What are you looking at, huh?"

Fatass seemed to be trying to crawl into himself, like a turtle without a shell. "Nothing," he said, and jiggled away after Edgy. The guy, he didn't even look at me again. He just got in a sleek yellow Barracuda and squealed his tires, pealing out.

The O was beside himself. I'd never seen him happier. He helped me up and brushed me off as the crowd wandered away. "Hey, man," he said, "You woulda kicked his ass. That guy, he was doing Edgy a favor. You see him scare the shit out of Fatass? Man, I never seen someone go from being so tough to so wimpy so fast since Man Mountain Cannon turned into Crybaby McCarthy." O was talking so fast I could only half hear him. I was still trying to slow my heartbeat down some to get it out of my throat, breathing in and out, tasting a little blood from a fat lip.

We were both so worked up, we just started walking any which way. I mean, really stepping too. The O, who usually waddled, was striding like a pro. We even ended up down on Dallas. One of the Earls was working on his car in the street, grease smeared across his forehead. He didn't say a word. After a while, I noticed the O's empty hands. "What about Animal Farm?"

"Forget it," he said. "I'll make something up."

We stopped down at Shaw Park and sat on the swings, smoking and laughing, replaying and modifying the story. O picked a long blade of grass. "Should have given old Edgy the Hindu. I bet those muscles of his would have just about exploded," O said, tensing up his body and contorting his face. We both howled.

"I never seen that guy around the house," I said, "but he knows Larry. I owe big brother Larry big time."

O, who had no brother, liked hanging around my house when Larry was home. It was like he had a crush on him or something. Larry, a champion rocker, had graduated and was working in the plant with my dad. He was five years older than me, and we'd never been very close.

"Yeah, you owe Larry, that's for sure," he said. He started really swinging, up and down, pumping his arms, then he did the craziest thing for a big kid like him to do: he jumped off and landed in the muddy grass. He bounced up, limping a little, but laughing, laughing uncontrollably.

That night after dinner, we met under the streetlight for our evening prowl. O and I had a route we liked, our little circuit for smoking and walking and shooting the shit. Every night we passed by the old Ryan Theater, which had closed the previous year. The marquee out front still read CLOSED FOR REPAIRS. Or C O F R R RS. Kids had started busting out the glass and knocking down the letters when it was clear the Ryan was never going to reopen, like most of the businesses in our neighborhood—everything was moving out to the suburbs. That night, we were surprised to see only one letter left.

Somebody'd been busy. Neither of us had a very good arm, so we hadn't knocked any letters down with our few furtive attempts. This looked like our last chance.

"Sure would like to have that," he said.

That one letter was an O, and right then, I knew I had to get it. I picked up a handful of stones, and, when no cars were coming, zinged them up against the marquee. I slung one handful after another while the O nervously kept watch. Finally, I nicked the edge of it, and it swung, then fell slowly down. The O reached out, and, though he bobbled it and it hit the cement, only a small piece chipped off. He handed it to me, not presuming.

"Hey, it's yours—a Big O for the Big O."

"Thanks, man," he said, holding it tight, raising it above his head. "O, O, O," I chanted, dancing with him till we were choking with laughter, oblivious to the passing cars.

After that, we didn't want to press our luck—we'd had enough of our little dreams fulfilled for one day. We headed back toward our street and sat on the corner of Otis and Pearl where the streetlight was burned out. The same streetlight Carl Minski crashed his car into when the cops were chasing him. You could still find little pieces of windshield glass in the street and in the grass around the pole. We called it Minski glass. The O was scooping his hands along the curb, as if panning for gold in the piles of dirt that always accumulated there. He sifted in the dark until he pulled up a tiny square of safe-tee glass.

"A rare piece of Minski glass," he said, "a little red. Maybe some dried blood on it."

"Bullshit," I said, "you can't even see it." Though that was a lie. It twinkled in the rare clarity of moonlight. Some nights it seemed like our city rained broken glass, and then there were nights like that, where it seemed like we were getting the last good pieces of everything.

"Ruby-red Minski glass," he laughed. I punched him in the shoulder, but I was laughing too. It was nice that we could sit together in the dark like that. Tomorrow would bring more taunts of "shlurpee" and "big boobs." Hell to pay for a lost *Animal Farm* and a battery charger that didn't charge. But that night, the O had his O, and I had been rescued by the Barracuda Man, as we would come to call him, even later, when he pumped gas down at Jack's and wore a shirt that said "Bobby" on it, though we knew his name was Ray.

He reached over and put his arm around me—something we just never did. "Hey Timmy," O said, "we make a great tag-team." I looked at him, and he looked at me. At that moment, I felt the world was nearly perfect. "Get away from me, you homo," I said, but I didn't move his arm away. He just grinned.

Eventually, he got that car, and we aimlessly circled the streets. It was no better than walking, really. We stopped walking, and we stopped wrestling. And we had nowhere to go—that was our biggest sadness. We could only eat so many Belly Busters. The factory did swallow us both up, briefly, then we fell into the murky water of layoffs and lost each other. We held our breaths and bobbed to the surface in the fresh, clear waters of love and decent money.

Years later, when we both lived far from that dirty city of our births, far from the broken glass of everything that seemed important then, O wrote to tell me he really was gay. We'd lost touch, but he wanted me to know. I had a feeling that might be true on the night of the Barracuda and the red plastic O. And he must have known it then too, though it'd be years before he'd admit it to himself, and to his crazy parents, who then wrote out new wills to disinherit him, though his father was only a janitor and his mother had nothing to her name. The Big O. He wrote that he felt like kissing me sometimes back then, but pushed that thought away like a bad dream. "I didn't know then that it was really a good dream," he wrote. He had a friend. They lived together, and he was happy. "Or at least an okay dream."

He was my best friend who knew I was a coward. In my heart of hearts, I loved him, I surely did. That night walking home, I stopped and turned to watch him lope up the steps toward a house identical to my own. His steps buoyant. Nearly floating.

34 ⋄ Jim Ray Daniels

Black Box

Something bad was orbiting in ever-smaller circles. Closing in, and Bob knew it. Just yesterday, a hawk swooped up out of the hollow just inches above his head while he crossed the bridge on his way home from work. A small scare, but definitely not *it*, not the thing that was coming. He almost welcomed the small scares, their brief surges of electricity. His life was so boring lately, he was thinking about changing his name, or at least giving it a new twist. His middle name was Raymond. Maybe he could be Bobby Ray Miller, from the South.

Last week, a plane taking off from the airport crashed outside of town in the Allegheny River, killing everyone aboard: 138 people. Unlike the hawk, the plane could not rise up over a bridge. They were still finding pieces of it, pieces of them, in the river, the woods. It made him sick. Made everybody sick. Bob wished he knew someone on that plane so he could have a deeper reason to grieve. A friend's father was on it, and his cousin's boss, and his girlfriend Annette's childhood friend. Today, as he walked across the bridge again, though he knew he shouldn't, he was grieving for his own name, that stupid, plain name.

Bob worked in the Pittsburgh Conservatory as a gardener. They told him what to plant and where, and he did it. Just once, he wanted to do some arranging of his own. He had some ideas. At home, he grew vegetables in straight even rows. No flowers. Flowers were his *job*. Annette worked in the conservatory gift shop. He'd been seeing her for three years, and they'd settled into a comfortable boredom together.

"Hey Babe," he said as he stepped through the door. Annette was putting on her navy-blue smock behind the cash register.

"Hi Sweetie." Even their pet names were the usual.

"How'd you sleep last night?" he asked. She'd been having trouble since the crash. Annette hadn't seen her friend, Terri, in fifteen years, but she'd cut out the obit photo and carried it in her wallet.

"Good. Okay. Pretty good." She forced a smile. She looked worn with worry, her eyes sunk deep where Bob could not reach. The gift shop always smelled like potpourri, dry and phony. Bob thought it should smell more like wet dirt—the possibility of growth that drew him to this job thirteen years ago.

"Maybe you should see a doctor?"

"Oh, what do *you* know?" she suddenly snapped at him.

Fred Whitcomb, the conservatory director, walked in just then. Bob shrugged and hurried off to the tiny locker room to change into his overalls. A rumor was circulating that the city was going to privatize the conservatory because it was losing money. That made Fred, and everyone else, a little jumpy. Bob wondered if that would be his tragedy—losing his job. Just a little tragedy—he could handle that. What he would do, he had no idea, but as long as no one died, it'd be a relief.

His alcoholic uncle fell out of his row boat and drowned last month. Bob never cared for the man, so it didn't count. One of the volunteer flower ladies keeled over from a heart attack at her daughter's wedding six months ago. That's what started it—every month since, he felt it closing in. Now, the plane crash. The hawk.

Changing into his overalls, Bob noticed Fred behind him.

"Robert, I'd like a word with you before you get started." Larry and Jack, the other gardeners, finished dressing quickly and left. Jack rolled his eyes at Bob as he passed.

"Mr. Whitcomb," Bob said, nodding. "What's up?"

"Robert, I was wondering if you could do a job for me. An extra job. I'd pay you double your hourly wage."

Bob stopped snapping his overalls. "What'd you have in mind?"

"My dog. Would you bury her for me?"

Bob started snapping again. His heart plunged into muddy swamp water. Bury a dog? That's what his boss thought he was good for?

"I can't do it myself. My children, they want her buried on our property. I have a bad back." Fred rubbed his back as if it were aching just that second. He couldn't be that much older than Bob—maybe forty-five. Fred was well-off enough to have "property." Born into it, everybody knew. The director's job didn't pay that much, but it was a respectable job for someone from Fred's world.

"Oh, man," Bob started. Why me, he wondered, because I dig a good hole? Fred wouldn't even know what a good hole was.

"Listen," Fred said. He adjusted his tie. Some guys played with their crotch when they got nervous. Fred adjusted his tie. Bob was listening, but Fred seemed to have forgotten he was talking. Bob coughed.

"Listen," Fred said, "I'll give you a flat fee—$100. It can't be more than two hours work."

Sweat trickled down under Bob's arms. One reason he took this job was so he wouldn't have to sweat like that—sweat squeezed out from under somebody's big thumb. "When did it die?"

"Cancer's eating her up. Vet can't do a thing."

"You mean, it's still alive?"

"Yes. The children won't let me put her to sleep, but she could go any day now. I want to be ready. We want to have a nice burial. It's just, the mechanics, putting her in the coffin, all that. I'm attached to the dog. I just can't do it." Bob thought Fred might cry, but he just adjusted his tie again.

"You've got a coffin? Geez, okay, I'll do it," Bob said. His heart was blowing bubbles up from the slimy swamp bottom.

"I'll call you when I need you." Fred turned quickly and left the stuffy locker room. He had never come back there before. Jack and Larry would be sure to want to know the story. The truth was too weird. Bob would have to make something up. He pulled at his crotch. He grabbed his shovel and wheelbarrow and went to work.

One of the few times Bob had talked to Fred, he made a suggestion which Fred shot down. Bob liked trimming the topiary animals, but what drove him crazy was the artificial carrot stuck in the rabbit's paw.

"Mr. Whitcomb, what about using a real carrot in there? That fake carrot is falling apart. The styrofoam's showing. It makes the whole thing look cheap."

"Listen," Fred said, pausing to look at Bob's name tag, "Listen, Robert, we can't afford to be buying bags of carrots for a fake rabbit. That seems pretty absurd, doesn't it?"

"Not to kids. Not to kids, it doesn't. I can't tell you how many kids I've seen say something about that fake carrot. It's filthy. It doesn't even look like a carrot anymore."

"Robert, you should be spending more time gardening and less time listening to people—that's *my* job."

"And I'm telling you what they're saying. I don't see you...." Bob trailed off. He didn't want to be a complainer like Larry and Jack. Fred walked away. Bob started bringing in his own carrots, a new one every week. He kept the old fake one in his locker, just in case somebody complained, but no one ever did.

Larry and Jack gave him a hard time.

"Hey Bobby, going to feed the rabbit today?"

"Rabbit looks a little hungry today, Bobby. Gon' need a new carrot soon."

Bob suspected Fred asked him for help because Bob had a reputation for going along with the program, whatever that might be. Not like Larry or Jack. "Gardeners with Attitude" they called themselves, and even had t-shirts made up. They gave Bob one. He took it, but he never wore it, not even at home. They held their tools like weapons when the office staff passed. Annette hated them.

"I went to school with guys like them," Bob told her. "They're okay." He'd grown up in the city, where his father had worked in a steel mill. Intent on not following his father, Bob had gone to a rural two-year college where he majored in forestry, then came back to the city to work in the conservatory. His father had died of lung cancer two years ago. He'd never stepped foot in the place—hated the whole idea of it. "Rich old ladies sniffing flowers," he scoffed, "and my boy dancing in the tulips for 'em."

"I get as dirty as you ever did," Bob always told him, as if dirt was a sign of something. "Yeah, for half the pay too," his father replied, and that was true. But Bob loved his work, loved wandering the conservatory's quiet green paths. His father could never say that about his own job. Today, Bob was working in the Fruit and Spice Room. It smelled like a peaceful dream.

That night over Annette's, they watched a special on the plane crash, and it made her cry.

"Those poor people," Annette said as she turned off the TV. They sat in silence. Usually, they'd make love after the news, then Bob would either spend the night if it was a weekend, or go home if it was a work night. But not tonight—not since the crash. Sadness hung in the air like the musty smell in an old person's house. An old person who was dying. Annette took out the picture of her friend again.

"She was a nurse," she told him, as if that fact clarified her grief. It clarified nothing for Bob—the crash had unsettled everything between them. Maybe if he'd just known someone on the plane.

"Yeah, you told me that before," he said. In the paper, they'd listed the dead, with brief bios of all the victims.

It was the kids that made Bob saddest. Those short lives made for short obits. He thought about what his own would say: "Bob Miller, gardener." Then what? People would skim right over his name, he knew.

"So what if I did? You're pretty cold sometimes."

"She was married, but no kids." Bob said, though he knew Annette had the bio memorized.

"I wish we hadn't lost touch," Annette said.

Bob felt like she was talking about them. He wanted to comfort her, but felt hesitant, awkward. It was like they were suddenly on a first date again.

"Did I tell you about that hawk I saw yesterday?" he asked her.

"Yes, you did."

"Oh. It was something. Beautiful."

"I can't think of anything flying without thinking about that plane."

"Even a bird? Even a beautiful bird?"

"Even a bird," she said angrily.

"Hmmm." Bob said. He wanted to leave, but not too suddenly. He didn't want her to think he was leaving just because they weren't having sex. It was something else — he felt dizzy, as if the room itself could crash.

"You know, I love you. I need you," he said out of the blue.

She paused. He waited for her to say it back to him. "I love you too," she said finally, but she was staring at the blank TV screen. "I hope they find the black box," she said. They were still searching the murky waters.

"Me too," Bob said. "Maybe it'll explain all this."

On his way home, Bob rolled down his window and let the cold air rush in. They were both thirty-five. She'd been married once and divorced. He'd never been married. Their families and friends were impatient for them to get married, or at least move in together. Bob wondered if they were too old for either option. Too something. Or not enough something.

Bob wanted a child of his own. It was an absence, a growing hole in the silence of his life. At work, he smelled the rosemary and dreamed of a daughter he would give that name to. Rosemary, sweet Rosemary. Annette said she was too emotional to be a mother.

"It'd tear me up," she said. "every time it cried, I'd cry. You know me, Bob."

"You'd be a perfect mother," he'd tell her, though he had no idea. He knew he wanted to hold his child with clean, scrubbed hands and smell its new hair and sweet breath.

Getting dressed for work the next morning, Bob nearly cried watching the weather channel. It all seemed bleak. He felt sorry for the weatherwoman trying to be cheerful, pointing bravely at the dark clouds. Storm front moving in, and didn't he know it.

The next few days, it seemed like Fred was ignoring him—not that he ever paid him much attention. Bob twice saw him veer off when they were headed toward each other on the same path. Then he saw Annette veer away from him too. After work, he found her just as she was raising her smock over her head.

"Hey," he said. "Maybe we should go on a trip together. Some kind of vacation."

The smock mussed her curly black hair. A few gray ones in there too. She looked like she just woke up. Her eyes startled Bob, and he took a step back.

"How can you think about a trip after what happened?"

"Oh. Yeah—the crash. Well, we can drive," he said. "I didn't mean fly somewhere. That'd cost too much. I mean somewhere like Myrtle Beach for a few days. It shouldn't be crowded now."

The last week in September, and leaves were starting to change. They'd just opened the Fall Flower Show, for which leaves had been brought inside and strewn on the paths. Bob thought that was crazy, bringing leaves indoors.

They didn't teach him anything like that in forestry school. He knew who'd have to rake them all up. Raking indoors. That was the kind of thing his father would've made fun of.

"No. No, I don't think so....In fact, I think I need some time alone. This crash, it's got me rethinking everything."

Bob kicked at the indoor leaves with his boot. She was grabbing her purse. He walked beside her out the door.

"Everything? Everything, like us?"

She didn't say anything. Her head was darting back and forth like a bird's, like she was waiting for someone, looking for something.

"Damn, and I was just getting ready to ask you to marry me." He threw that out to get her attention.

"You don't mean that," she said. She wouldn't look at him, which was fine with Bob. She suddenly seemed enormous standing beside him.

"Maybe I do. Tell me about this rethinking."

"I'm not done yet," she said. "This weekend. This weekend, let's talk."

"I might have to bury a dog this weekend."

"What?" she said.

"You just never know," he said, and stopped on the sidewalk as she walked the last few feet to her car. On his walk home, three planes flew overhead. Bob looked hard at them all as they smoothly crossed the sky.

She never called that weekend, and neither did Fred. Bob called her, but she wasn't home. He tried to change his name tag to read Bobby Ray, but he smeared ink all over it. He didn't wear a tag to work on Monday. *Bob*, he thought — what a stupid name.

That morning, he was restless, and the green paths did not offer their usual solace. He was hiding in the topiary room in the cool darkness under the little bridge when Fred tracked him down. Bob thought he was in for it. What work could a gardener be doing in a tunnel? But the tunnel suited Fred's purposes.

"Where's your name tag?"

"I forgot it. Besides, you know who I am," Bob tried to joke. That was the problem. Everyone knew who he was. He hadn't surprised anyone in a long time.

"Any day now. Maybe tomorrow. I can't stand it. The dog's suffering. The kids. I just might have to do it. To take her in, have the vet put her out. You free tomorrow after work?"

"Yeah, I'm free. Free for a hundred bucks."

He got the call later that night. Fred was whispering. "I think she stopped breathing. I can't hear anything. Can you come over now?" It was nine o'clock. The weatherwoman standing in front of the giant maps looked bravely confident as she predicted rain for much of the Midwest.

"Where do you live? Where is your...your property?"

In half an hour, Bob pulled up the circular drive in front of a depressing gray stone house. Not quite a mansion, but with the pretension and ornaments of wealth. It reminded him of the conservatory.

Fred was standing outside in front of a row of neatly trimmed bushes. He motioned Bob to follow him around back.

As they circled around to the garage, bright floodlights crashed into his eyes. "Motion sensors," Fred whispered.

Bob stumbled and fell against Fred. Fred instinctively pulled away, and Bob fell to the ground. Fred gestured at him. "Hurry up."

Bob knew it was all wrong, him being there. This was it, he felt. This is the thing that was coming. In shadow on the side of the garage, a springer spaniel lay on its side.

"Are you sure it's dead?"

"I...I'm pretty sure. When I call her, she doesn't respond."

"What's her name?"

"Queeny."

"Queeny, hey, Queeny," Bob called. Nothing doing. Bob bent down and felt the dog's chest.

"She's dead," he said.

Fred was starting to breathe funny, like he was choking. Bob realized he was crying.

"I'm sorry," Bob said.

Fred let loose and began to sob. Bob put his hand stiffly on his shoulder.

"Hey, c'mon, you don't want to wake up your kids now, do you?"

"She, she was a good dog."

Bob looked up at the sky and sighed. He didn't have the stomach for this. His job was to help things grow. It was starting to rain, splattering on the dead dog, on Bob's glasses, on Fred's shiny black shoes. Bob gently lifted the dog. I'm holding something dead, he thought, and his scalp tingled.

"The shovel's in the garage, and the coffin," Fred said, trying to pull himself together. "But I don't know," he said quickly, "Maybe I should let the kids see her dead. What do you think?"

Bob stopped. Fred was asking his advice. "Hell, I don't know. I don't have any kids. I'm not even married. In fact, I might not even...." Bob paused, trying to shake off the spell of the dead dog in his arms. "You've got the coffin. Why not just show them the coffin, tell them she's in it?"

"Yeah, that's it. Just show them the coffin. They've seen her. They know how sick she is. Was." Fred was blowing his nose. Bob set the dog down.

"Well, I'm here. What do you want me to do?" Bob asked. He wondered where Fred found a dog coffin. It was about the size of a young child.

"Oh, damn it....Just bury her now. Dig the hole and put the coffin in."

"Okay. I'll take care of things. Uh, by the way, do you have the money?"

Fred quickly produced an envelope.

"How much is in here?" Bob looked levelly at Fred.

"A hundred, like I said."

"Where's the spot?"

"The spot?"

"Where do you want the hole dug?"

Fred led him back near the line of trees at the back of the yard. It was darker there, where the motion sensors could not reach.

"I can't even see," Bob said. "This is crazy."

Fred giggled nervously. "Yeah, it is, isn't it. I panicked a bit this evening....But you're here."

"Yes, I'm here." Bob laughed, despite his anger. "Got a flashlight?"

"No."

"Man, I don't know. Poor dog. Why not just take him..."

"Her," Fred interrupted.

"...her to the vet and have the vet do whatever he does with dead dogs....What do they do with 'em anyway?"

"I don't know. That's why we wanted the burial. To keep her here with us."

"How about your headlights? Can you pull your car back here a ways and turn on your lights?"

Fred sat on the hood while Bob dug. The spade was brand-new. To Bob, it seemed all out of whack with the plane crash to be burying a dog like this, but Fred's grief seemed real. He had to respect that.

"How many feet down? Not six, I hope."

"At least a couple."

Bob took off his jacket. He was sweating through the polo shirt he wore. He figured that's what guys like Fred wore to be casual, but Fred still had a button-down shirt on under a cardigan. The soil was good here. Not much clay.

"Deep enough?" Bob panted as Fred looked down.

"Is it ever deep enough?" Fred asked, then quickly said, "Yes, yes, it'll do."

Bob placed the dog in the coffin. Fred touched her side once before he closed the lid and Bob lowered it into the earth.

"Want to say a prayer? Do the first handful?" Bob asked.

"What? Okay. Yes, sure. You must think I'm a little cuckoo," Fred said. *Cuckoo*—Bob laughed to himself and shook his head.

Fred tossed a few clumps of dirt on the coffin, brushed the dirt off his hands and made a quick sign of the cross.

Bob suddenly wasn't sure Fred had a bad back at all. He looked around in the headlight's glow and wondered who did the gardening there. He quickly shoveled the dirt back into the hole. Fred disappeared and came back with a small stone cross. Bob pushed it into the ground, thinking of all the crosses going up for the crash victims. What merits a cross? Bob wasn't a churchgoer. What kind of loss merits a cross? He pushed it in till it was firmly planted.

"I'll finish up here. You go on in now," Bob said to him.

"Please, Bob, don't mention this to anyone at work."

"Fred, I was just going to ask you the same thing," Bob replied.

"Yes? Yes."

Bob reached out to shake on it. Fred hesitated, then shook Bob's hand firmly. "Our little secret." Bob wasn't sure, but Fred may have winked at him. Fred pulled his car back and shut off the lights, then hurried into the house. Bob was happy to be back in darkness. Walking to his car, he tried to avoid the sensors, but they nailed him with light.

At work the next day, Bob was stiff and tired. He wasn't used to digging holes that late, that deep. Outside, everything was dying. Inside, the dirt was moist, and plants were blooming. Bob needed this job more than ever. At closing time, he ran into Fred.

"How are you today, Robert?"

"Fine," Bob said. "Fine. How are the kids taking it?"

Fred twisted his mouth up into what looked like a smirk and walked away.

Bob stepped out the door into the first wind with winter's name on it. He hunched inside his jacket and started walking. A helicopter heading for the hospital roared overhead. He'd avoided Annette all day. He knew what she had to tell him, but he didn't know if he was ready to hear it. Eventually, he'd have to go over and pick up some clothes and things at her place. Three years was probably long enough, he told himself. Maybe someday they'd be friends and eat lunch together now and then. Each time he spotted her now, though, his scalp tingled. He'd been hiding in the rain forest exhibit for hours at a time, taking deep breaths of moist air.

When they found the black box, the pilot's last words were simply, "Oh shit." When it came time, it was Bob who swept up the leaves so they could get the Christmas Flower Show ready. He tried out Bobby Ray on a few people, but it didn't really fit. He was a Bob—no getting around it. He started carrying a piece of manure in his pocket because he liked the smell, and people left him alone. He started taking bites out of the topiary rabbit's carrot, so that by the end of each week, it was just a nub. He spent Fred's money and got himself a dog from the Animal Rescue League. He named it Shirley, after his favorite weatherwoman. She had such a hard job, trying to predict.

In December, the heating pipes broke in the Cactus Room and killed many of the plants. Others sagged with brown leaves, dark spots. Everyone who worked at the conservatory gathered to survey the damage. Annette, Fred, the Gardeners with Attitude. They stood in silence as snow bounced off the glass above them. It was just one room in one conservatory, and not everything died. But Bob *knew* these plants, and his eyes began to blur with tears. Fred surprised everyone and put his hand on Bob's shoulder. Annette rushed out of the room. The Gardeners with Attitude cursed the faulty pipes.

Annette called him that night. "Are you alright? I've been thinking about you."

"Yeah, yeah, I'm fine." Bob nodded into the phone. He hadn't spoken to Annette since they'd had their official break-up. "I'm fine," he repeated.

"Let's have lunch sometime," she said. "....Got to get you out of that rain forest," she joked.

"Yeah, that's what I've been thinking," he said. "I've got a dog, you know," he said.

"That's nice," she said. "They'll get some new cacti."

Fred laughed. He could never call them cacti. Made him think he was talking Greek or Latin or something.

"Good to hear you laugh," she said.

"I'm always laughing," he said, though he felt tears rising again, so he quickly said good-bye.

One morning in January, he looked over the bridge on his way to work and saw a crumpled body lying on the ground far below. He stopped and stared down. It was always cold on the bridge in winter, the wind blasting through the hollow like a train. The paramedics were just arriving. It was clear, even from the bridge, that they needn't hurry. Bob had been eating a donut, and it fell from his hand over the railing.

The paramedics looked up when it hit the ground. Bob shook his head and started walking again. He looked up into the empty sky and thought about that hawk he'd seen last year. It was beautiful, soaring up above the steep hills squeezing the hollow. It wasn't just one thing closing in. It was every day, always, pressing against the glass. He put his head down and picked up the pace. He was going to work, where he helped things grow.

All Packed

Jim Ray Daniels

Andy had no idea where they were. It didn't matter. He stared out the window at the dark houses. The streetlights poured their pale blue light into circles on the road in front of them. Detroit copied itself over and over—this street was the same as a street five miles over—Eight Mile Road, Nine Mile Road, Ten Mile Road, all the way up to 32 Mile Road. The square, boxy houses, schools, grocery stores, the cinder-block bars, tool-and-die shops, and the long, flat blur of factories.

He turned back toward the three women in the car. In the back seat, Cindy and Debbie were lighting up cigarettes. Linda was driving. He leaned over and pressed his head against her shoulder. She shoved him away, laughing, "You can't be tired now, can you, big boy? What do you think, girls? Looks like we picked us up a deadbeat."

"Five years ago, he wouldn't be pooping out on us like this," Cindy said.

"Five years ago, you would've kicked my ass out of your car by now," Andy laughed.

"Five years ago, we wouldn't have even let you in the car," Linda said.

"Five years ago," Debbie said, and trailed off. He'd danced with her at the reunion. They'd joked about kissing at a junior-high party.

"Ain't that the truth," Andy said. He reached into his pocket, flicked a couple of antacids from the roll and popped them in his mouth. He watched two teenagers standing near the curb under a street sign sharing a cigarette or a joint. They stared at the passing car with that scared defiance Andy remembered having.

Linda was taking them to Debbie's for coffee—no one wanted to go home. Stan Edwards had planned a post-reunion party at his new house, but he'd gotten sick on the drive there, so his wife sent everyone home. Andy used to call him "buy six—drink two" Edwards, though the whole thing about who could drink the most didn't make much sense anymore. Now who couldn't measure up? Andy closed his eyes. He didn't even have a job. Tomorrow, he was leaving town to look for work down south. His car was at his parents' house, all packed.

He'd gotten a ride to the reunion with his old pal Zack, who'd left early, so he mooched a ride off Linda, with Debbie's help. He was sure Linda and Cindy thought it was funny having him in the car with them—Andy, the old burnout.

"Sure you don't want us to take you home?" Linda asked.

"No, no. I could use some coffee," Andy said. He was embarrassed to still be living at home. He'd never really moved out, except for his brief, half-hearted attempt at college. He was in no hurry to get home now. He wasn't up to facing his parents and the morning's move.

Andy leaned again toward Linda, this time to turn up the radio—an old Bob Seger song, "Ramblin' Gamblin' Man."

"Wasn't our class song a Seger song?"

"Yeah. Not this one. It was 'Turn the Page.'"

Andy turned toward the back seat to look at Debbie. "You're right. I think I voted for some partying song—I don't remember."

"I'm surprised you remember anything from senior year," Cindy said.

"Hey, c'mon, I wasn't wasted *all* the time...."

Andy tried to stick to beer as a rule, but tonight the old fears crept back, and he'd needed to beat them off with some stiff drinks. He was stuck with how people saw him five years ago, and stuck with five more years he wasn't proud of on top of that. He'd had to answer too many questions about flunking out of college. When it had happened, it seemed like a joke, but now he could only swallow hard and shrug, "I guess I just wasn't ready."

"Despite tonight, I don't drink much anymore. And I quit drugs. Even pot."

"It's okay, Andy, we believe you," Debbie said, and patted his shoulder from the back seat.

"I bet some of those guys are eating their hearts out right now, wishing they were single again. And me, here with three beautiful women...."

"They can always get divorced," Debbie said. She'd married pregnant the year they graduated. Had two kids and was now divorced. He turned again to face her. "Sorry," he mumbled.

"No need." She smiled.

He rolled down the window and let it slap his face. He was playing the fool again, but he didn't know how to stop.

Andy had gotten a girl pregnant in high school, but she'd had an abortion. A secret he'd told no one. She'd been there tonight with her husband, and he'd meant to at least say hello. Once, he'd started toward her table, but whatever song that was carrying him that way ended, and in the quiet lull he pulled back, turned around. They'd both been drunk, and getting married and keeping the kid was never an option. Her parents took care of everything. Why would she want to say hello to him now?

Debbie had been quiet for most of the ride. She didn't fit with Cindy and Linda, college grads, professional women. They pulled into Debbie's driveway. She'd gotten the house in the divorce. And the kids. The principal had kicked her out when she started to show. Later, she took night courses to graduate.

The father of her children, Richard Wood, had been a basketball star two years ahead of them. His father was a school board member, a barber who called himself "the drug buster" in his election materials. They were both known as Woody. Debbie confided to him at the reunion that Woody Sr. had made trouble during the divorce. "A real mess," she said, shaking her head slowly through the smoke from her cigarette.

Andy followed the three women into Debbie's house. The kids were with her mother for the night. He bounced up the steps, energized by the strangeness of this group, something different at last.

Debbie held the door open. As he passed in behind the others, she whispered, "I don't remember much myself, since they threw me out."

"What?"

"Senior year. I don't remember much."

"How'd you end up with those two?" Andy whispered.

"We grew up on the same street. I think I'm their charity project. Their mothers probably made them ask me. I didn't want to go, but my mom offered to take the kids. I don't get many chances to get out."

"Are you glad you went?" Andy leaned toward her.

"Let's go in. I'll get that coffee going."

The other women were both headed toward successful careers. Debbie was stuck here living on child support, her future tied down by two strong ropes. In high school, she was as smart as any of them, as beautiful as any of them. A strange combination of passion and compassion surged through Andy.

"So, Andy, what happened at college?" Cindy asked as they settled around the kitchen table. Andy shrugged.

In the awkward silence, Debbie pulled out pictures of her kids. The absence of music, after a long night of it, settled uncomfortably into the air. Andy slurped down two quick cups of coffee till he felt his heart pounding. He had a headache. He chewed a couple more antacids, then went into the bathroom and searched the medicine chest. He found some asper-gum and popped a couple pieces into his mouth.

"This one's Katie, my oldest." Debbie smiled, pointing to a somber girl alone on the porch. "And here's Katie with Bobby." Two years apart, they stood with their heads leaning into each other, a man's hands on their shoulders.

Cindy was talking about her job, her transfer back to the city, the condo she was buying. Andy remembered when condo wasn't a word. He felt Debbie's foot moving up his leg. He looked across at her, and she smiled. He flipped off his shoes and stretched his legs out under the table. She squeezed his feet between her thighs as the others talked, their words fading into a muffled rise and fall.

Andy wasn't dumb. He'd simply made no effort, stumbling stoned down the long, noisy hallways of their high school. He had nothing as tangible as Debbie to point to as an excuse for his failures, yet she herself offered no excuses, took pride in what she had: her children. He'd clearly wasted the last few years.

He wondered why Zack had left early. He'd been talking about the reunion for weeks. When they'd arrived together, some guys had kidded them about being a "couple." Old reliable Zack, still living at home, just like himself. He lived for bowling, and bowled on three other teams besides the one he and Andy were on together. Zack had more seniority in the plant than Andy because he'd started in straight from high school, so he still had a job. He liked living at home, and his parents liked having him. He weighed close to three hundred pounds.

Andy was glad they hadn't gone out to breakfast with the others. He felt like enough of a failure right here. Cindy would be moving home to clerk at a local law office. Linda had an extra room in her condo. They were making plans. His plan was simply to drive away. He had two thousand dollars saved. It would have to do.

Debbie caressed his feet, which had stopped moving. He began stroking her thighs again. He felt like he was at someone's house whose parents were away for the weekend, and he was worried they'd come home early and shut the party down.

"When I get out of law school, I'm gonna kick some ass. Big bucks." Cindy laughed at her own display of bravado. Andy was sure she'd make a great lawyer. All through school, she did everything right. Teachers loved her. She had always intimidated Andy—she exuded the strength and confidence that he never had. In high school, they were miles apart. Now, it seemed like light years.

"Where were you when I needed some ass-kicking done?" Debbie asked as a joke. It silenced the others.

"Well, you got the house," Linda finally responded, exchanging glances with Cindy.

"How come you're not a lawyer, Linda?"

"You wouldn't believe how many people ask me if I'm a lawyer yet. Shit," Linda held a cigarette to her lips, stamped it red with a kiss, "the assholes don't even know how long it takes to become a lawyer....The kind of money I'm making now, who needs it?"

"How long *does* it take to become a lawyer?" Andy asked. Across from him, Debbie smiled.

"Hey, are you two playing footsy?" Linda asked, incredulous.

Andy reddened, despite being drunk, despite knowing he shouldn't care.

"Safe sex," Debbie laughed. "It's been a long time. I have to start somewhere."

"Maybe we'd better get going."

Debbie moved her foot up Andy's crotch. He was humming to himself. He wanted more coffee, but his gut was hurting.

"Coming, Andy?"

Debbie squeezed his feet. "No...no, I think I'll stay awhile. Debbie will take me home...I think."

She laughed. "Eventually."

Cindy and Linda looked at Debbie, then at each other. Cindy shrugged. "Fine."

Debbie quickly locked and chained the door behind them. She turned, and Andy met her immediately with wet, hungry kisses. They were starting to undress each other when the doorbell rang.

She froze. "Go in the other room, quick." Someone was pounding hard, and Andy knew it wasn't Cindy or Linda. He hurried into the bathroom and sat on the edge of the tub. When he heard a man's voice, he locked the door and wedged his feet up against it.

"There's someone in there with you, isn't there?"

"Woody, it's none of your business. We're divorced now, remember? What do you *want*?"

Want, Andy said to himself. He wanted to pee, but he was too scared. He hadn't been in a fight in years, and Woody was a big dude with "drug buster" blood. Andy tried to open the bathroom window, but it wouldn't budge. Woody must've been watching the whole time, Andy thought—probably has a gun—saw us come, saw the others go. They were arguing loudly. He heard the chain rattle, tried to remember a prayer. He hadn't been with a woman since forever, and now this. He spat out the asper-gum.

"See, there's no one here. Now will you leave?"

Andy breathed into his shirt and shut his eyes.

"Okay. But I'll be back."

The door slammed. The chain rattled back into place. Andy couldn't believe it. Woody'd never been very bright. Maybe he hadn't seen them after all. He heard Debbie sigh, then heave into tears. He was sober.

He stuck his head around the corner, then awkwardly put his arms around her where she sat on the floor. After she calmed down, he asked how long she'd been divorced.

"Six weeks....Oh, we've been separated over a year. I don't know what his problem is. He must've found out the kids were at my mother's and suspected something. I mean, he doesn't love me anymore—he's told me that. He's just not ready for anyone else to love me, I guess."

Love, Andy thought, oh man. She wiped her eyes and pulled Andy down to her, kissing him fiercely on the mouth. They hurried upstairs, stopping on the landing to shed their clothes. She tackled him onto the bed. The phone rang. She let it ring, but her kisses slowly faltered.

"I have to answer it," she said, pulling away. "It might be something about the kids."

It was Woody.

"Why won't you leave me *alone*? Just let me live my life," she spat, one word at a time. "We'll talk about it later." He called three more times, then, finally, gave up.

They made wild, clumsy love, like high school virgins, and it was over quickly. Afterward, they lay still and quiet in the bed.

"What do you want?" she asked.

"To try it again."

"After that?"

"I don't know." Andy rolled over onto his stomach. At the reunion, he'd only made jokes when anyone asked him what he was doing. The sky was gradually graying into light. He closed his eyes—the long drive, to who knows where, was filling his head with panic and pain. He blurted out, "I'm leaving town tomorrow. Driving south to look for work. My car's all packed up."

Debbie looked at him blankly.

"There aren't any jobs around here. My unemployment's just about run out. I still owe money on my student loan...." He let his face fall forward, and he groaned into a pillow. She put her arms around him tenderly.

After flunking out of college, he'd gone to work in the plant with his father until getting laid off a few months ago. College was his own fault—just like high school, he tried to party his way through. His own fault, his parents often reminded him. Wasted their hard-earned dollars. After a few years in the factory, Andy had no doubt that they were hard-earned. He was tired of hearing it.

"Do you ever think about leaving here?" he asked suddenly.

She laughed. "Woody's dad would track me down. Besides, I got my kids....I love my kids....Do you ever think of going back to school? When the kids get older, I'm going to try."

"That's a great idea," he said, ignoring her question. "You were always smart."

"Not always," she said. "You were pretty smart yourself, till you started getting wasted all the time." She punched him hard in the shoulder.

He kissed her then, and they made love again, slower this time, almost sad. They both stank with the smells of a long night—whiskey, sweat, smoke, coffee. Exhausted, he buried his face between her breasts.

She shook him gently—the sun was up. They'd slept for such a short time, he wondered if he had imagined it. She got up and went downstairs to make coffee. It was morning no way of getting around it. He dressed slowly, then followed her down. He had the shakes. She held him against the kitchen counter, staring out the window over his shoulder. He slumped in a chair sipping coffee while she showered and dressed.

"I have to pick up the kids in an hour," she said.

"I have to leave town today," he said. He'd put off leaving because he'd promised Zack he'd go to the reunion. Seeing everyone getting on with their lives was just what he'd needed to harden his resolve. His uncle had written him from Houston to say he could find work there. It sounded as good as anywhere. He wondered if getting laid off might turn out to be a good thing. During the long, slow months of unemployment, watching bad TV while his parents nagged him, he realized he had to get out of there. And the factory work, well, maybe he could do better.

He knew his parents must be ready to kill him. Staying out all night another example of his refusal to take responsibility for his life. He figured they expected him not to leave today, to come home and sleep it off, to blow off another day of his future, and he had to admit, that sounded good right now. The night with Debbie was something to sleep on. The way he was feeling now, he'd be lucky if he made it as far as Toledo.

"Are you glad you went to the reunion?" he asked.

She smiled and kissed his neck. "Yes," she whispered in his ear. "You?"

"The reunion, I don't know about, but these last few hours. I'm glad I came here."

Andy looked for signs of Woody before emerging from the doorway and hurrying to Debbie's car. Even though Woody still had his factory job, Andy felt sorry for him. He had a family to support and was living, Debbie said, with his parents for the time being. Andy thought of his father's bitter laugh, the factory embedded in his hard stare, and his mother's weary silence, her sighs of disappointment. Goofy from no sleep, he felt hot tears welling up in his dry, burning eyes.

The leaves were turning, some falling. His stomach was on fire. Toilet paper hung from some tree branches, that old high school prank. They passed from subdivision to subdivision, past their old school, the corner store he used to work at. He tried to shake off the tears with a sharp laugh. Debbie held his hand, her eyes holding to the road. He wanted to break out, leave the rotten children of his past on the doorsteps of this barren town.

Andy rubbed his eyes and took a deep breath as she turned down his street. His parents, dressed for church, were getting in their car. Debbie parked in front of the house. He kissed her good-bye. His hand trembled a bit as he wrote her phone number down. His parents ignored them. Debbie reached across the seat and buttoned a button he'd missed. They both smiled. He kissed her again as his parents pulled out of the driveway, then he slipped out of the car.

"I'll call next time I'm in town." Debbie squeezed his hand through the open window, pulled him to her again. "You'd better," she said.

"You've got it tough, Debbie. Hang in there." Even as he spoke the words, he realized how lame they sounded, how much he suddenly felt toward her. "I *will* call," he said. "From Houston, or wherever." She had to pick up her two kids, then have it out with her ex-husband, but now, she was smiling. He let go of her hand, then walked up the steps, turning to watch her drive away, then heading into the house. He showered, changed, wrote a note, ripped it up, wrote another, longer note, then walked out the door. He started his car and drove off. At the expressway, he turned south. A light rain fell. He drove on for miles, then, finally, turned on his wipers.

Tunnel to Canada

Angela and Bill stood in front of the sculpture in Hart Plaza as if they had just crash landed. The sculpture, a long, twisted piece of metal, part of the wreckage. Despite the clear day, they were lost in the morning haze of their separate hangovers.

"So, what about some pierogis?" Bill asked. They'd come to Detroit for Bill's brother's wedding and had decided to go to the Polish Festival down by the river.

"What?" Angela was looking off to the side at some boys with their shirts off playing in a fountain.

"Pierogis. Those little dumpling things my mom makes." Bill rubbed his forehead and squinted into the sun.

"Food. That's all I need," she groaned.

"It'll make us feel better. We'll work it off dancing polkas." Last night, they'd stayed up after the rehearsal dinner drinking shots and beers with his relatives. Bill was going to be the best man.

"Sure, let's be lovebirds and dance together," she said. She put her arm in his, so he decided she was sincere.

They walked past a small band of ragged musicians hacking away at "The Beer Barrel Polka." The accordion player was a tattooed skinhead. No one was dancing. Angela rolled her eyes, "What's this, punk polka?"

Bill performed an exaggerated, jerky dance in front of her, and she gave him a playful shove. Further on, a row of food booths led to the main stage where a larger group dressed in Polish costumes played in front of a crowd of enthusiastic dancers.

"Bet you don't hear too many polack jokes around here," Angela laughed.

Bill nodded and smiled. He liked her when she was like this, when they were alone together and sober, and she shared herself directly, only, with him. Children in bright costumes wandered through the crowd, punctuating his sudden good mood. They bought pierogis at the Knights of Columbus booth and washed them down with their first beers of the day.

It was cool for August, and a breeze blew across the river from Canada. He'd never taken Angela over—she was afraid Customs would find a stray marijuana seed or lift some cocaine dust from deep in the carpeted floor mats. The thought of crossing over made him nervous too. At the border, declarations had to be made.

This would be their last weekend together. When they returned to Bowling Green, Bill was immediately moving to Los Angeles to start a new job. He felt like much of the tension between them had been, if not removed, then forgotten, by the trip to Detroit. Their lives had been yanked one way by his impending move, another by her inability to finish her dissertation. She was supposed to be done by now. The new plan was that she'd join him out west when she finished. Neither of them had known how much tension the dissertation would cause.

Lately, nearly every night began with a vow of peace and ended with them both drunk, back to back in bed, curling tight around their own angers. He closed his eyes for a moment and pictured her drunk. Would that be the image he'd take to California with him? Angela, eyes slit open, face pale and puffy, dressed in the ragged jogging suit she wore around their apartment?

* * *

"Well?" Bill stared at the computer screen in front of her at the kitchen table. All he could see was the blinking cursor.

"Don't start on me already. Jesus Christ, how can I live with this shit?"

"If you didn't work, did you cook? I'm hungry." He smiled tightly. The daily disappointment of the blank screen was wearing them both down.

She yanked opened a beer can, spraying foam in his direction. It spotted the stack of books beside her. Angela had come to Bowling Green because it was her father's alma mater. He had a doctorate in chemistry and was vice president of a large chemical company in Denver. She had worked as a waitress and gone to school when the feeling moved her, once taking a year off to be a ski bum with an old boyfriend. She'd finally gotten serious when her father threatened to cut her off. It had taken her five years to get her B.A., and now she was trying to hang on for the Ph.D., even though she had little hope of finding a teaching job. Why she'd chosen sociology was now a mystery even to her.

She worked hard for a couple of years, but now that she was close to thirty, everything was slowing down again. She took out student loans and spent the money on drugs. Her department seemed more eager to get rid of her than she was to graduate. As long as she was in school, she could maintain the illusion of future potential, of fulfilling her father's expectations. It seemed like *everyone* had their expectations, all crowding in around the kitchen table.

In the fridge, seven beers were left from a twelve-pack that hadn't been there when Bill had left for work. He shook his head, grabbed one for himself. "Did you really put away five beers already?"

"That's a good boy," she said as he popped the can. "Remember, a sandwich in every glass."

Bill remembered—he'd used that line to justify his drinking back when they were both students. "We're going to rot in this shit-hole town, I swear."

"I wish we could afford some drugs."

"Maybe we can, once I start making big bucks out west." He winked at her, but she just shook her head, forced a loud burp.

Bill met Angela when he was a senior and she was finishing up her Master's. He'd begun in pre-law and ended up in business. He couldn't find a job in his field, so he worked on the line at the Oldsmobile plant in Toledo while Angela finished up. Now, he'd finally landed a job in business. He had assumed Angela would graduate in the spring. He'd even got his starting date postponed, still hoping she could finish. He couldn't put it off any longer.

"Let's go to the Bird tonight. Jenny and Jim are down there," she said.

His eyes caught hers, held. "You sure you need any more?"

"Fuck you, are you coming?"

"Fuck you, are you coming," he aped, but drained his beer and followed her down the steps.

She wondered if she'd ever go to California. It seemed like a surrender. Even though she now depended on Bill financially, she still pretended to be living off loans. She'd already used up her limit on fellowships and her father's patience. They were drifting apart, and sometimes she just wished it was over—for him to be gone, across the country. Other times, she found herself still clinging.

She loved Bill, but the dissertation had brought out a meanness in him—using money like a weapon, just like her father. Each day she sat paralyzed, hoping if she just sat there long enough, maybe everything would work itself out without her.

At a back table in the Bird, they sat with Jim and Jenny, two other grad students. Angela leaned across the table, telling one of her Colorado stories. The others were laughing. Bill turned his chair around to watch the pool players. His quarter was next up on the table, but he was getting antsy, ready to leave. He had his hand around his glass on the table behind him, and he felt it suddenly cool. Angela had filled it and was raising the empty pitcher to order another. He wasn't drunk enough to forget about morning, and the factory.

"Hey, Angela." He paused. Lately, when they went to the Bird, they had the same argument, the one about whether Angela was going home with him or staying. Usually, Bill lost. Tonight, he didn't care. "I have to go home." He drained the full beer, dribbling a small stream over his chin.

"What a man!" Angela said with mock reverence, holding her hands over her chest. But she pulled him back toward her when he stood to leave. "Are you really going?" He thought she looked scared, or maybe she'd been priming herself for a fight and was disappointed. He kissed her quickly, nodded to the others, and headed through the smoke toward the door. On nights she stayed out, Bill had trouble sleeping, knowing she would stumble in later to ask him to hold her or to continue the fight.

Now that he was done with school, Bill felt like an outsider at the Bird. He didn't understand the departmental gossip and the long, circular discussions of research methods and case studies. When he talked about *his* work, they looked away, or headed to the john. He thought they should be interested in his stories, being sociologists. He had written a paper for Angela on sex roles and sexual stereotyping in the factory. She got an A on it, which made her angry and made him think the dissertation shouldn't be so hard.

Walking down the street toward their apartment, Bill imagined them back in the bar making fun of the way he'd tried to guzzle his beer. He thought the others egged Angela on for their own amusement. They probably made fun of her too when she wasn't around. They didn't seem to care whether she got her degree or not. Despite the graduate student rivalries and factions, Angela seemed to get along with everyone. One thing about Angela, she could be a lot of fun at a party. Maybe no one considered her a threat. He wished she could see he was the only one really on her side. That night when she came home, she didn't wake him, and when he woke for work, she was sleeping beside him, still dressed, her legs jerking as she wandered lost in a dream.

* * *

Strolling between the rows of vendors, Bill was spotted by Mrs. Linowski, who was working the Polish Century Club booth.

"Yoo-hoo, is that you, Billy Wysocki?"

He stopped. Angela poked his ribs and whispered, "Bill-eee, someone's calling you-oo." She smiled as he reddened. He turned, "Mrs. Linowski? Hi, how are you?"

"Oh, Billy, so good to see you." She pulled him over the railing and hugged him to her, imbedding her "Kiss Me, I'm Polish" button into her chest. "Oh, you look so good!"

He smiled weakly.

"You know," her voice lowered, "My Cindy's getting divorced." She shook her head. "You were smart to wait. Is this one Polish?" Bill nodded, though it wasn't true. She turned to Angela and raised her voice, "And who's this?"

"This is my girlfriend, Angela. Angela, Mrs. Linowski."

"Hello, dearie."

Angela looked at Bill, then back at Mrs. Linowski. "Hello."

"Did you know Billy used to call me Auntie Helen?"

"No, no I didn't." Angela smiled, the corners of her mouth turned up into a bit of a sneer.

"Yes, and he dated my Cindy for the longest time."

They bought kielbasa sandwiches from her and stood chewing and looking around till Angela tugged on his arm. "We've got to move along. My brother Steve's getting married tonight, you know."

"That's right, and you're next. Well, good-bye, Billy. Good-bye, Dearie. You take care of Billy."

"Angela."

"Yes, good-bye." Her smile faded, then flashed again as she turned to another customer.

As they walked away, Angela dug her nails into his arm. "What's with this 'girlfriend' bit? And 'dearie.' How'd you like that for a mother-in-law?"

"She's a lot like *my* mother. What's the big deal? You know my parents are embarrassed about us living together. I couldn't think of what else to call you."

"We've been through that before."

"Yeah, and we never came up with anything that sounded right."

"What about 'lover'?" she spat the word.

Things had gotten so bad, he wondered if that would be any more accurate. "A little too racy for Mrs. Linowski, I think."

Angela seemed combative, and he didn't feel up to arguing. "Did you hear her say Cindy's getting divorced?...My high school sweetheart."

"I hope she doesn't have her mother's nose."

"Well..." Bill had to laugh Cindy did have her mother's big honker. Angela showed the trace of a smile. He felt relieved—maybe they wouldn't fight. He wanted to do something to stop this floating apart, to have fun today, tonight, until he left. He wanted desperately to store up some good times now to try to cancel out the fighting. Once she finished, and they were alone together in California, far from these hard months, maybe things would improve.

"What do you think of Claire?"

"She seems nice enough, but so goddamn mushy. She reminds me of a toothpaste commercial the way she's always smiling, hanging onto Steve. I never hung all over you like that, did I?" She parodied Claire's smile and snuggled suggestively up to Bill, rubbing her head against his chest.

"Sure you did. And it doesn't feel too bad now either." He gave her a sloppy kiss. "Anyway, Steve loves her."

"Steve doesn't know shit about love. He's just a kid. Like you." She grinned.

"And you do? Are you the love expert?" Bill held her tight, laughing as she struggled to get away.

"Why don't they just live together?"

"They're serious." He released her. "They want to settle down and have a family."

He looked back at the spray from the fountain tilted by the wind. "I used to think about getting married—who'd be my best man, all that stuff."

"I hope this wedding business isn't rubbing off on *you*?"

"Why not?" he blurted out. "Why not get married?"

"These are awful, you know." She was eating a gwumpke he'd bought for her.

"Just a little cold....What about it?"

"I bet your friend Cindy could tell you a few things about the wonders of marriage....You're just worried because you're moving."

"*We're* moving, right? And what's wrong with security? I'm tired of this craziness. California's too far away."

"Why'd you take that job, then?"

"That was the deal—I'd stay here till you finished, then you'd come with me where I got a job."

"Yeah, yeah....Well, I'm not finished."

He hung his head and kicked the ground.

"Poor Billy." His head rose and he stared at her. "C'mon, knock it off," she said, grabbing his hand.

"Yeah, let's drop it."

They walked past the last booth and out toward the main stage, where they stopped to watch the dancers. An older couple in front of them glided by, faster, more graceful than the rest. "Look at them, aren't they good?" He wanted to be able to dance like that when he was old, to know someone else's movements that well.

Angela nodded, put her arm around his waist. "I do love you. But—what am I going to do out there?"

Bill grabbed her arm and pulled her into an open spot right in front of the band. The accordion player was introducing the next song. Bill looked over Angela's shoulder at him. He winked, and Bill smiled back. He tried to lead her into the flow of the music as the song began. She wasn't ready and stumbled against him, then grabbed him tightly to make him stop.

"Let's start over."

Bill sighed, then began again. He wished they could start everything over, wished they could dance their way through the invisible resentments blocking a clear path in any direction. They were still out of step, but Bill kept moving, bullying his way, hoping to will them into harmony. Maybe they belonged with the other band, the one they'd passed playing off to the side. "How come we can't do it?"

"Because you're doing it wrong!" Angela shouted above the music.

"I'm a polack—I *know* how to polka." Bill hadn't done it in years, but it was a simple dance. Angela shook herself free and began pushing through the crowd of happy dancers. Bill grabbed her arm again.

"Hey, I'm sorry. Let's start out slow and try it one more time."

"Maybe we need a couple drinks first."

"No, c'mon, let's go: one-two-three, one-two-three, one-two-three." They seemed to be getting it, so he gradually sped up, but as they twirled around, he stepped on her toes.

"See?" She threw up her hands.

"See what? You're still doing it wrong!" Now, she was running away. He began weaving through the crowd behind her.

"Angela! Angela!" He was trying not to yell—people were staring. He could see her headed toward the river, but he couldn't wrestle himself free.

When he finally reached her, she was sitting on the cement embankment, staring down at the water. "I'm sorry. I really am." He reached down and pulled her up. "The way we've been drinking and fighting lately...." He hugged her tightly, and they stood together for a while until she pulled away and returned to the water's edge. He held back a few seconds, then moved down to join her.

"Remember the first time I brought you home with me and you saw the Tunnel to Canada sign and thought it was the name of a restaurant or something?"

She smiled. "Yeah, that was funny....Why build a tunnel when you already have a bridge?...I'm from Denver, what do I know?"

Bill shivered in his t-shirt. Evening was coming on, and they'd have to get home soon. The polka music, distorted by the wind, sounded funereal. They both stared across at Canada. They'd been in love then, when the Tunnel to Canada sign could have meant anything. Now, they were only a couple hundred yards from its entrance and could not pretend.

The bridge or the tunnel—that was the choice every time you crossed the border. One way or another, Customs waited on the other side. "Do you think they'll be like us in a couple years?"

"Your brother and Claire? Sure."

Bill was thinking of the toast he'd make at the wedding. He picked up a loose piece of cement and threw it in the water. Cabin cruisers littered the river. He didn't know what to say. "Wouldn't it be fun to own a boat?"

"They look like a bunch of jerks."

It was true enough, Bill thought, with their silly hats and sunburned beer guts, honking their loud horns. He could picture his brother, a hot-shot car salesman, looking like those men on the boats in a few years, but not himself, and that made him feel a little better. He kissed Angela's hair and moved tight against her.

"Where's your romance? How about a nice sailboat on the Pacific?"

"Romance never got me anything but trouble."

"C'mon, you don't mean that. Why do you always have to act so tough?"

"Look at that asshole." She pointed down the river to a man pissing off the side of his boat. Bill thought about being drunk. "I don't know," she said. They sat in silence.

"I don't think you're ever coming to California," he said softly, almost glad to have spoken the words at last.

She said nothing. The wind was strong, and he wasn't sure she heard him. He didn't want to say it again.

"You don't want to marry me," she said. This time, he was silent.

"Let's try to dance again," she said suddenly, "out here."

"I can barely hear the music," he complained, slowly getting to his feet.

"Come on," she said firmly, and grabbed him, "One-two-three, one-two-three, one-two-three." They started carefully, Angela leading. They were dancing better now, away from the crowd. As they picked up speed and began circling, Bill started to get dizzy. "Stop dancing and hold me," he said, but she wouldn't stop.

Jim Ray Daniels

Shooting a Few

Jim Ray Daniels

They stood together outside the car. Andy pointed across the lot to the two basketball courts near the tennis practice wall spray-painted with graffiti.

"There they are."

"Yeah, I know. I go to school here."

"Yeah, yeah, I know you're in high school now. I was just saying, 'there they are' — not like you hadn't seen them before. Just 'there they are.'"

Andy tossed the basketball in the air and tried to twirl it on one finger. It spun for a second, then fell to the ground, splashing in a small puddle. They walked over to the courts, Andy in front, Joe, his girlfriend's son, behind him.

"A little wet," Andy commented, stepping around another puddle in the uneven surface of the blacktop, "from the rain last night."

Joe was looking at the practice wall. Andy scanned it, looking for Joe's name, or his name, some other Andy asserting himself, but he found no names that he knew. He wanted to touch Joe's shoulder as a small sign of affection. The obscenities on the wall, the gray sky, the puddles, all contributed to Andy's vague sadness. His father had always shaken hands, never more — never an embrace, never a gentle touch. Andy didn't know how he would ever reach this kid.

"Earth, calling Joe." He held an imaginary microphone to his mouth. They stood on the empty court. Joe looked at him, and Andy tried to read his face, as if they were already playing, one on one. "You ever shoot out here before?"

"No. The only time I ever played was in gym class. I told you that."

"Yeah. Well, apparently, your mother thought this was something we could do together...."

"Apparently."

"And have some fun." Andy couldn't believe how grown-up the kid sounded. He was fourteen, and there wouldn't be room for another adult anywhere in his heart for at least ten more years, he guessed. "I like your mother a lot." No response. He dribbled the ball on the dry spots.

"No getting around that. Like her a lot.....This is called dribbling....you probably know that."

Joe rolled his eyes and looked away. He was short, a bit heavy, and he had bad acne, the big, hard, ugly bumps. At that age, Andy wanted nothing worse than a girlfriend. He had one now. He still wanted nothing worse, desired nothing more intensely than the love of a woman. The way Joe looked, it'd probably be awhile before he had any luck. Andy stuck up a tentative jumper from fifteen feet. It hit the rim, bounced away toward Joe.

"For some reason, your mother must've thought you like basketball."

Joe looked him in the eye. "No, I think she was just desperate. She knows *you* like basketball." He bent down and picked up the ball. Andy splashed his foot in a puddle. They were stuck with each other, at least for the afternoon. It was starting to sprinkle again.

"Shoot it. Let's see your shot."

"No. Let me watch you. See the master at work."

Andy looked again at the boy, who half-heartedly tossed the ball to him. It landed short and splashed him. He picked it up and dribbled around, took a hook from the free-throw line. It jingled through the chain-link net. He laughed, surprised. "See that?"

Joe was watching two girls ride by on bicycles. They wore light spring jackets, their faces bristling against the cold rain. It was late March, and like most years in Michigan, winter was grimly holding on, no matter what kind of jacket you wore. Joe wore a baggy old army jacket which hung nearly to his knees. Andy was wearing his old varsity jacket, which now stretched tight around his waist. The ghost of the letter—F for Ferndale—showed itself as a lighter spot surrounded by grease.

Andy put up a bank shot from the side. It bounced off the backboard, hit the rim, and fell in. He was starting to loosen up, even sweat a little. He ignored Joe and started playing a game of Around the World with himself. When he was a boy, Andy shot baskets to cure whatever was bothering him—teachers, girls, family troubles. All through high school, as he became more and more confused about everything else, shooting baskets in the yard against the rotten wooden backboard became his refuge. Had he told Elaine, Joe's mother, this?

He remembered shooting under the floodlight in the rain the night his grandfather died, his parents watching from the kitchen window. He didn't go in until all the lights in the house were out. It was tough when there wasn't anybody to blame, when there wasn't one clear reason for somebody dying, for somebody falling out of love, for your parents going their separate ways.

He shot all the time back then, and after a while, he became pretty good at it. He played varsity for two years, then quit in the middle of his senior year when the coach told him to get a haircut. Andy laughed out loud, remembering his own stubborn stupidity. He held the ball above his head, watching imaginary men cut across toward the basket. He faked right, went left, pulled up and shot a fadeaway jumper from the corner. Air ball. Andy sighed and forced another laugh.

"Shooting baskets is one of the simplest things in the world," he shouted to the boy, slightly out of breath, "trying to put a ball...in a hole."

"If it's so simple, why can't you even hit the rim?"

"It's the *trying* that's simple. I mean, you know what you have to do. The goal is clear." He paused. "What interests you, Joe? What's your idea of a good time? You seem like you're against everything."

Joe didn't answer. All he ever did when Andy was visiting Elaine was watch TV. Andy couldn't recall it ever being off except when he was in bed with Elaine and wished it were still on to cover the sound of their love-making. He dribbled in and shot a fancy reverse lay-up. He was falling into the old easy rhythm, the simple joy. Joe was getting the rebounds, tossing the ball back out to him. Andy hoped he was feeling it too, at least a little bit, at least vicariously.

"I don't want you to marry my mom."

Andy stopped dribbling, tensed up: free-throw time.

"Listen, I know this will take a while. I'm not going to replace your father or try to compete with him." He had rehearsed this speech with Elaine. "It's only natural for you to resent me. *I'd* resent me if I were you. If we marry, that means your parents aren't going to get back together. Ever. I know that's hard to accept."

"I think I heard that speech on TV once. I don't *want* them to get back together — they fought all the time. I just don't like *you*. I don't want to live with *you*...." Joe looked as if he had more to say, his face distorting into fear and anger, verging on tears, but he remained silent.

"Well. You told me, didn't you," Andy said. His neck burned, even as he tried to remain calm. It was no use. He wasn't going to change his whole personality to suit some pimple-faced kid. This was their fourth outing without Elaine, and each had gone progressively worse. Pumped up, Andy drove in hard for a lay-up and nearly dunked it. At first, they had both seemed to be making an effort, but now the kid was apparently giving up.

"Here. Your turn to shoot." Andy drilled the ball across the court with a baseball throw. The startled boy put up his hands and knocked it down. "Ouch," he said. Andy coughed up a gob of phlegm and spit it out into a puddle. "I mean it," he said. The threat in his own voice frightened him. He didn't know the first thing about raising kids. He felt the anger of catching someone cheating. He sat down hard in the wet grass at the edge of the court.

Joe held the ball in his hands, staring at it like it was a pimple he was thinking about squeezing. He turned to Andy.

"Okay. You want me to shoot, I'll shoot." He marched into the wet grass behind the backboard and tossed the ball back up over it. It sailed beyond the front of the rim and bounced toward Andy, who picked it up and threw it back to Joe. He shot backwards again, and this time the ball hit the top of the backboard and bounced down into his own hands. A third try made it over and hit the rim. So did a fourth. The moisture from the wet grass was seeping through Andy's old gray sweat pants as he watched a fifth and a sixth shot both miss the rim completely. Joe's face flushed with the effort. Andy wished it would stop raining. He knew this was going to take a long time.

Seeds

Curt sat alone in the kitchen. He shook the packet close to his ears, then ripped it open and dumped the seeds on the table. He could hear Nancy breathing in the next room. His lunch bucket sat on the windowsill, a chunk of the black sky brought indoors. Sky pie, he thought and laughed. Sky pie for lunch. He looked at his watch: time for work.

Yesterday, he'd read in the paper how cantaloupes were luxuries in Japan, given in a special box, like candy, to sick people or to congratulate someone. He'd told Nancy about it while they were out grocery shopping.

"We can give them to all our friends," he told her.

"All what friends?" she answered. "Where's the shopping list?"

He noticed both her hands curled tightly into fists. "Hey, if you're not going to get in the spirit of this, forget it."

"No, no, I'm sorry." She put one hand on his shoulder, and with the other dropped a seed packet in.

"Green onions." She smiled.

"That's better."

They'd decided that making a garden was something they could do together. Five years, and the marriage was so shaky having kids was out of the question—long evenings of silent TV or drunken fights. And they were the perfect age for starting a family, Curt thought. She was twenty-nine; he was thirty-two. If the garden went okay, maybe they could think about it again.

Today was Friday, their usual night to go to the Tel-Star and wash down some payday beers. Curt worked as a toolmaker at Red Wing Gear and Axle, and Nancy worked as a security guard at the community college. At the Tel-Star, they got drunk and flirted around, then, usually, they fought. They couldn't seem to give up fighting, despite their peace declarations and cease-fires. One week it was a new sex book that only embarrassed them, the next, a marriage counselor Curt almost punched. This week, seeds, a garden.

As Curt sat fingering the seeds, he wondered about tonight. If he had to give a reason for the Tel-Star, it was that he liked the possibility of something happening, even if it meant another fight. He'd never cheated on Nancy, but he liked to get drunk enough to imagine it. The Tel-Star was getting old though—no one new to rub knees with under the table.

"The guys at work think gardens are for wimps, can you believe that? I bet I could go up north and bring down a pickup truck full of farmers to show them different."

"Oh, you're such a natural man, Curt."

He didn't know how to take that. She'd been in this sarcastic mode for the last month or so, and he wasn't sure he liked it. Maybe she got it from the students at school, or from the other cops.

"What about beans?"

"Beans, yeah."

"Carrots?"

"Carrots, yeah."

Saturday, they were supposed to plant the garden, and he knew if they got drunk tonight, they wouldn't do it, might never do it.

He hollered over his shoulder toward the bedroom, "Ready to plant tomorrow?"

No response. He looked at his watch, then peeked in the bedroom. The covers were off, and she was naked. He bent down and traced a line between her breasts. She slapped at his hand and frowned.

"What are you doing?"

"Getting ready to plant."

"Ha. You mean, *Go* to the plant, don't you?"

Curt tried to think of an answer both witty and playful. He just snorted, and patted the bottom of her foot on his way out. "See you later."

"Yeah. Later."

At the Tel-Star that night, Curt sat at their usual booth waiting for Nancy. Frank, the owner, nodded, and his hair fell down into his eyes. He combed his hair up and over his bald spot and looked a little like Shemp from the Three Stooges.

"Where's Nancy tonight? Ain't she coming in?"

"Probably not."

Frank put the beer in front of Curt and headed back to the bar. He was one of the guys Nancy flirted with, and Curt didn't want to give him the satisfaction of expectation.

The jukebox was playing Frank Sinatra. At least it wasn't "New York, New York." The Country Travelers came on around ten. They played watered-down country-pop that Curt liked to dance to after a few beers. He prided himself on being a good dancer, sometimes practicing in the mirror at home when he was alone. Some nights, when drunk enough, he'd do the leap-and-spin move that used to wow them at high school dances. Some of the bar patrons called him Mr. Leap-and-Spin. He didn't know how to take that.

Curt started making a list of who they could give cantaloupes to: his mother, his brothers. Nancy's folks. Ernie and Ben from work—no, he thought, they'd just laugh. No neighbors. A lot of them had young kids now, so Curt and Nancy were outsiders on the street. Next door, Ed and Judy hadn't spoken to them since the basketball incident.

Curt had always dreamed of putting up a hoop in his yard once he bought a house. Last year, he finally did, then invited Ernie and Ben and their girlfriends over one night to christen it. The men were still shooting at ten o'clock when Ed came out of his dark house and started watering his bushes. He stood by the side watching them while his hose sprayed any which way.

Next thing, the police were there. Ed's bushes were soaked, but he wasn't going anywhere.

"Come on, officer," Curt complained, "Can't a guy shoot hoops in his own yard? It's not that late. It's a weekend."

The younger officer took an outside jumper and swished it. The older officer frowned and turned to Curt, "You musta been yelling a lot or something." He looked around the corner at Ed watering his bushes, and Curt realized who'd called the cops.

"The young one's kind of cute," he heard Nancy say.

"Ed, I'm going to have to kick your ass," Curt said, and took a few menacing steps toward him.

Ed sprayed the hose at him, then Curt really lost it—rushing at Ed and throwing wild punches till the cops separated them.

The basketball hoop was like the garden idea—something to keep him active. To keep him from moping around. To keep him from drinking. To help him and Nancy. She'd played ball in high school and still had a decent shot. He'd always kidded her about playing a game of strip "horse" before he put up the hoop, but after that first night, he rarely used it, and when he did, he played alone.

"After the ruckus with the cops, you think I'm going to go out there and have all the neighbors critiquing my shot?" Nancy told him.

She walked in the bar and sat down across from him. "Happy payday," she said. Frank brought her a beer, pronto.

Curt sat in the booth writing down names, crossing them out, penciling them back in while they drank and waited for the place to fill up.

"Now, what do you think someone should do to get on our cantaloupe list, honey?"

"Don't you think you're a little ahead of yourself there, dude?"

"If they don't make the cantaloupe list, maybe we can put them on the carrot list."

"The carrot list? Who the hell'd want carrots as a present? Listen, Curt, let's just plant the damn garden and see what comes up....Hey Frank, how about another beer?"

Jenny, the waitress, dropped two beers down, giving Curt one he didn't ask for. He quickly drained his old beer, and she took it away.

Curt sat silently with his pencil, drawing carrots and cantaloupes next to people's names. Even if he didn't actually give anyone carrots, in his mind he could categorize them as carrots. He realized how few people he was close to. The cantaloupe list was padded, definitely padded.

Ernie and Ben were carrots-and-a-half right now.

He'd met Nancy in a bar, and what first caught Curt's attention was how she could put it away. She kept up with him drink for drink and never seemed to get shit-faced. Funny thing was that now Curt couldn't keep up with her, and he wasn't sure he wanted to. The day-long Saturday hangovers were doing him in. The friends he had were drinking friends. The wife he had, a drinking wife.

Ernie and Ben and Ben's girlfriend, Sarah, squeezed into the booth with them.

"Looking good, Nancy," Ernie said.

"You're down to a carrot," Curt said.

"What?"

"Just ignore him," Nancy said. And they did. Curt felt a knee rub against his under the table. He looked around at Sarah, then at Nancy. No one returned his gaze. Somebody must have made a mistake.

Saturday morning, Curt was awoken by a car door slamming. He pulled his dry lips apart. His body was warm, like he had a fever. He slowly turned his head—gray outside, too early to be awake. Nancy wasn't there.

"Got to plant tomorrow," he'd said to Nancy. But he

didn't smile or wink or touch her as he got up to leave the bar.

She'd never come home. He lay in bed, stunned and afraid, until he heard keys rattle in the door. The storm door blew open. His body shook. He closed his eyes and pretended to sleep. Nancy went straight to the bathroom. The water ran for a long time.

He got up, threw on his jeans, and went out into the yard. The cold dew numbed his feet. He hugged his bare chest.

He took a shovel out of the garage and began turning the soil over. For the seeds. For their possibility.

Nancy slipped out the back door holding a laundry bag full of random clothes and toiletries. She was pale, her makeup smeared. She walked toward him.

"I'm gonna be a Country Traveler," she slurred.

He winced—a goddamn Country Traveler. She'd spent the night with someone in the band. Maybe the whole band, for all he knew. A bunch of young punks in their little white cowboy hats.

She picked up the basketball from the garage floor and took a set shot—air ball, though her form was good. The ball crashed onto their aluminum awning. A light came on in the kitchen next door.

"Hey," he said, "Why don't you go in and get some rest before you take off like this. We'll talk about it."

"I can't keep my Country Traveler waiting," she said with a laugh that made Curt shiver. Then she was gone— into her car, and off. Still, he thought, it was just a one-night stand. Maybe there'd been some misunderstanding. The guy would probably laugh at her when she showed up with her things. But for now, she was gone. He leaned on the shovel full of cold black dirt. His cold skin was the pale red of a winter tomato.

When he'd read about the cantaloupes, Nancy was polishing her work shoes on some old newspapers. Curt could see down the front of her shirt. He wanted to reach over and cup one of her breasts, but he'd felt clumsy. Lately, he had to concentrate just to make a smooth caress. It was like his hands ran into bumps where there were no bumps. He'd wanted to make some stupid remark about seeing her cantaloupes. He said, "You know, I've been clumsy lately." She looked up at him and said nothing.

Curt went back into the house and put on a shirt. He sat down to eat and think about things. He got a cantaloupe out of the fridge that he'd bought to give to Nancy. A gift for after the planting they'd do together. He sliced the fruit in half, and as he scraped the seeds out, he realized that he didn't have to buy seeds. They came with seeds.

Jim Ray Daniels

Night Shopping

Jim Ray Daniels

Harrigan strolled down the aisle, leisurely tossing things into his cart—the generic section, and he was loading up: peanut butter, puffed wheat, toilet paper, tube socks. He made a wide turn down the dairy aisle, then suddenly swooped back the other way—Schroeder, one of his colleagues, stood paused at the ice cream freezers. Schroeder was a full professor in Harrigan's department. He was shopping with Marcy, a graduate student who Harrigan himself had found attractive. She was articulate, confident, sexy—smart enough to fend for herself, Harrigan hoped. Schroeder, one way or another, devoured whatever he desired or hated.

Harrigan tried to discreetly circle back, give them a chance to avoid him, but Schroeder would have none of that. He was in a position to flaunt, and he didn't want to miss an opportunity, Harrigan thought dolefully. Schroeder was bearing down on him, and in the huge empty store, there was no escape. It was as if shopping at 3 a.m. was a crime and Schroeder wanted to make a citizen's arrest.

"Harrigan, how *are* you? Going generic, are we?" he said, glancing disdainfully into Harrigan's cart. "By the way, I read that poem of yours in the journal showcase in the hall—quite interesting, hmmm." He was leering at Marcy. "I haven't seen any of your work in a long time."

"That was only the first page. They only copied the first page." Harrigan was up for tenure next month, and he understood the weight of Schroeder's last remark. "I can give you a copy of the rest. So you can understand it. The whole thing, I mean."

He hadn't meant to sound defensive. He nodded to Marcy, who grinned at him and rolled her eyes. He wondered what was going on between them, between them all this very minute. He was catching a chill from the freezers.

"You could, could you? Another page, you say? What's the longest poem you ever wrote?" In the antiseptic cleanliness of the store, Schroeder and Marcy both smelled like enormous cigarettes — cigarettes, and perhaps gin.

Harrigan thought for a minute. He was clutching his shopping list like notes for a test. "Two, three pages — I don't go for the long ones."

"Oh? Well, on a scale of one to ten, how important is it for a poem to rhyme?"

"Zero," Harrigan said quickly, staring longingly at the cheeses. He was sure Schroeder, a composition specialist, hadn't read a book of poems in thirty years, yet he'd be filling in his low numbers on Harrigan's tenure ballot in a few short weeks, confident in his judgment, smug with his own ignorance.

"What do you think makes a poem *bad*?"

"Clichés, sentimentality, poor personal hygiene."

Marcy giggled. Harrigan wondered how long this could go on. He'd smoked a bowl of hash, as was his custom before grocery shopping.

"Oh? Well..."

"Well, indeed," said Harrigan. "It's on to the yogurt and cottage cheese then. Nice to have bumped into you here. A bit chilly, don't you think?"

Schroeder shook his head, as if he'd just cast his vote. Marcy was already walking away from them toward the checkout counter, holding ice cream and strawberries. She was doing her dissertation on the creative process and had interviewed Harrigan about his. The idea seemed to be to turn writing into a math problem. Harrigan studied expiration dates until he was sure the others had left the store.

He hadn't written anything in months. His book was "out" at half a dozen small presses, and all he could hope for was that someone would take it soon, very, very soon. He'd spent the summer in Toledo trying to sell used computers. Just trying it out, he'd told himself, just in case. The fantasy of getting rich and retiring early to write had always appealed to him, but it was clear that used computers weren't going to do it. He was seeing himself as more of a used computer all the time. It was frightening, how quickly they became obsolete, of no use to anyone. Now, it was back to teaching, the tenure decision looming, the darkest cloud he'd seen since grad school, when he'd lost his first wife to one of his professors.

At the checkout counter, Harrigan tried not to watch the cash register as the woman rang up his groceries. He wanted to think he trusted her. The other grocery chain had already switched to the scanner system. Whatever skill this woman had in pressing buttons would soon be obsolete. His total was over eighty dollars. He only had seventy-nine.

"That's okay," she said. "I can take off whatever you want."

Harrigan surveyed the groceries in front of him yet to be bagged.

"How about the bread?" she suggested.

"No, I need the bread. I eat a lot of bread. Sandwiches. Peanut butter and jelly. I'm hooked," he confided in a low voice. "I'll take the cashews back. Cashews—what was I thinking?"

She looked at him like a patient older sister might, though she was clearly younger. "We have peanuts for only ninety-nine cents." The cashews were his only snack item, his one luxury.

"No, no thanks. I've never done this before, honest. I usually figure it out right." Harrigan looked around: no one else in sight, though he heard a price gun shooting down one of the aisles. That'll be obsolete too, he thought sadly. He felt a bar code being stamped on his forehead, and he rubbed his temple.

"That's okay, don't worry. Everything is going up all the time."

"Except my pay check." Harrigan thought that was an appropriate response, one she could relate to. Though he was still making good money, he'd already calculated the number of remaining checks if he didn't get tenure: eighteen. "Have you worked the day shift here? On days, they'll make you run the gauntlet if you don't have enough money. I gave an old woman a dollar last month just to save her....I usually shop at night. More peaceful."

"You must not have to get up in the morning." She seemed bored with Harrigan, as if she preferred the silent hum of the fluorescent lights.

He nodded, then shook his head. She thinks I'm lying, that I don't even have a job, he thought, glancing down at his torn jeans, his paint-spattered shirt, the clothes he wore when he wasn't teaching. He did have on his best jacket, his drug dealer's coat, given to him by his second wife. Her old boyfriend had been a dealer and had left some clothes behind. Harrigan liked wearing the jacket—worn, brown leather. It made him look like anything but a college professor.

He handed his money to the cashier, his hand lingering over hers for a second: no ring. He stared at her name tag. They'd be getting rid of those too. *Lois*, it read. He hated that name. He always wanted to make a diphthong out of it. "What's your real name?" he asked. She looked at him, her head cocked. "I mean, your, your last name."

"Dilewski." She was loading up his groceries, stacking the bags back in his cart.

"Polish," he said, feeling like an idiot, feeling like he thought *Schroeder* should feel if he were only capable of recognizing his own inadequacies.

She looked at him, expecting more, expecting something like, "I'm Polish too," or "My first wife was Polish," which was true. She had picked up a pricing gun and was pointing it at him. "Do you know how many things I have to mark every night?"

Harrigan was suddenly ashamed of his preoccupation with his own fate. "No, tell me about it."

"Must be thousands—cans, bags, boxes—and they're all going up. Nothing's coming down. If they ever go down, it's only for a little while, then they go back up even higher." Her voice lowered, though they were still alone. "I worked at Cashway for three years before coming here. They accused me of stealing and fired me....a real mess. I lied to get on here."

Harrigan wanted to stay there, where it was light, and quiet, where this beautiful woman who was forced to wear a frumpy hot pink Big Valu jacket was being nice to him. Nice enough, anyway. Honest. In his world, honesty was a form of kindness. It was such a contrast to the day shift, with its cart bumping, shouting matches, and impatient shuffling in the long checkout lines. Harrigan felt like his whole life had become the day shift at Big Valu. He could never escape the aggressiveness of the people around him.

"That other guy who was just in here, with the young woman, have you ever seen him in here before?"

"I don't think so....Hey, are you some kind of detective or something? Did they send you over here?" She suddenly looked horrified. She ripped his last grocery bag, trying to squeeze it in his cart.

"No, no. I really don't even have a job. Do they have any openings here? I'm starting to get desperate."

"I hate these plastic bags," she said. "With the old paper ones, you could really pack everything neat. These plastic ones, everything just flops wherever it wants. No support, no structure." She dropped the ripped bag inside another plastic bag and this time simply set it on top of the cart. "Come in during the day and talk to the manager," she said with a small, uneasy smile.

Just then the automatic doors hissed open, and in came a homeless man pushing a cart full of empty aluminum cans.

"Sure, you bet. I hope I'll see you again. Thanks for your help. You really brightened my day. Well, I know it's night. You brightened my night. A little moonlight to help me find my way home...." Harrigan laughed at himself. "See, I'm a poet."

"Yeah, right," she said, rolling her eyes. "Goodnight," and she turned away from him. She had something to say to the man with the cans.

"Goodnight, Lois." He pronounced it as a diphthong, just to try it out. He wanted to ask her whatever happened to the "e" at the end of Big Valu, but he thought better of it and simply pushed his cart out the automatic doors and into the night. No support, no structure, Harrigan repeated to himself.

It was raining. Harrigan loaded the groceries in his rusty Escort and drove down the empty street, stopping at the light on the corner. A police car pulled up beside him. Harrigan knew he could turn right on red, but he froze until the light changed.

Back outside his building, he took out his keys. It was a quarter to four, and the street dripped with the silence of light rain. Mrs. Hesske, the widow who lived on the first floor, was asleep. She hadn't jumped up to turn the porch light off as soon as Harrigan had left the house, like she usually did, leaving him to fumble in the dark when he returned. It was a little game they played, and tonight he had won. "Ha," he said aloud.

He rustled his grocery bags, and the sound seemed amplified by the empty street. He imagined he was waking up everyone. A dog began to bark as he shut the door behind him. He set the bags down in the hall and reached up to turn off the porch light. He noticed a mosquito on the wall. October—a little late for mosquitoes. Harrigan scrutinized the bug, put his arm out for it to land on, but it seemed preoccupied—busy, busy dying. Putting the groceries away, he discovered that one of his eggs was cracked. He tossed it in the frying pan on the stove and turned on the heat.

A copy of the book Harrigan needed to get published was sitting on the floor in the corner of the kitchen like a pile of old newspapers. He was trying to save money so he could afford to be unemployed for a long stretch. He saw it coming, like Schroeder striding down the aisle toward him. Maybe he should have helped that mosquito out and smashed it against the wall.

He sat at the kitchen table. At Big Value—he'd put the "e" back on—they would call him Frankie. He'd become the favorite bagger of all the cashiers. Working nights, nothing would bother him. Nights when the police would come in to warm up and talk like anyone, nights when rain would streak the windows while he stood under the fluorescent tubes, sneaking kisses with Lois, shooting the price gun, marking things up through the long hours—*apples, peaches, pumpkin pie, who's not ready, holler. Just holler.*

No Pets

I gunned the engine, and my old Mustang II kicked up some gravel, shooting out of the Ritz's parking lot and onto Mound, a long, straight road full of factories and bars. The Ritz was a square, brick dive that filled a gap between two small tool-and-die shops across the street from my Ford plant. Drunk again. I swerved back and forth, trying to miss the potholes. At Eight Mile Road, a car full of high school kids turned right from two lanes over and cut me off. I slammed on the brakes and rolled down the window to yell, flip them the bird, but they squealed down a side street, radio blasting. I spent a lot of high school nights in cars like that. I cranked up my own radio.
    Back home, I parked the car in the street and headed toward the yard. I could already hear Bud howling, pulling against his chain. I hissed at him to shut up. He wiggled his butt and jumped in the air while I sat in the damp grass and unchained him. How could he still like me after the way I treated him? He ran in circles fast enough to make me dizzy. Bud was a pretty dog—white with black spots, sleek and alert to the world. His tail was cropped, and his whole butt wagged when he was happy, as if he was making up for what wasn't there. When he jumped in the air, it seemed as if he hung suspended for a moment or two, like a star basketball player. I was only twenty-nine, but he seemed to have a kind of energy I'd never get back. "Whoa boy. Come here." He almost knocked me down. "I have to get rid of you, Bud. Find you a good

home." He licked my face. I gave a factory howl and fell back in the grass.

"Hey, quiet down out there! And teach your dog to be quiet too!"

It was Turner, the owner of the house who lived on the first floor.

"What are you gonna do about it," I shouted back, "call the cops?"

"I just might." A window slammed shut. I turned back to Bud. "We ought to kick his ass, eh boy? One day I'm gonna."

Turner always complained about Bud's barking, about dog crap in the yard, paw prints in his garden. He said the dog was a nuisance, and maybe he was right. I knew I didn't give Bud enough time or attention. I didn't blame him for barking, for destroying things, for any of it. Turner had given me a week to get rid of him.

I usually had a few at the Ritz at the end of my shift, then drove home and slept, and in the morning I was tired or hungover, or both. I'd hoped getting Bud might help me break that routine, but even with him there, I couldn't stand being alone in that tiny apartment.

Turner was a young lawyer close to my age, but he seemed more like fifty. He was always dressed up, even on weekends, and talked like he was reading the news on TV. He drove a foreign car. His wife Lorraine was a nurse. They lived on the first floor and rented out the second to me while their "dream house" was being built out in Rochester Hills. People like Turner are always building dream houses—people who can afford to have dreams and fuck the rest of us over in the process. I'd lived in the house for three years. Turner had inherited it from his father, who'd never bothered me about the dog. He'd moved in three months ago after he kicked out the tenant on the first floor, an old retired guy from GM who had helped take care of Bud while I was at work. Though the first floor was bigger and nicer, I think Turner eventually figured out he got rid of the wrong guy.

I wanted to hit him, to bloody that perfect face of his, but I knew better than to hit a lawyer. Turner always got me mad—on the one hand, his superior attitude made me feel like dirt, and on the other, he was so slimy and phony, I felt like I should wash my hands after talking to him. And he always wanted to shake my hand. My father told me never trust a stranger who wants to shake your hand. That might sound unfriendly, but that's the kind of advice my father gave, and he was usually right.

I didn't want to talk to the cops, so I called Bud, and we went into the house together and up the stairs to bed.

* * *

I got up around noon and let Bud out, then sat on the porch drinking coffee while he ran free. I was thinking about Connie, a woman I'd met at my friend Boomer's wedding two weeks earlier. She gave me her phone number after we danced awhile, shared a few drinks. We kissed in my car afterwards. She must've been the only single woman there, and me the only single guy. "Fate," I told her all night, till she had enough drinks to start believing me. She was a phone operator and worked strange shifts too. She was sarcastic and sexy, and she made fun of herself in a way I wish I could do. I wanted to see her again.

I saw Lorraine Turner striding up the street toward the house, and I jumped up looking for the dog: "Bud, Bud, come here boy!" But he was already running down the street toward her. "Oh shit!" Bud jumped up against her thighs, and she pushed him away, patted his head.

"Hi, boy!" She glanced up at me on the porch—she looked like an angel smiling there in the sun in her white uniform, her blonde hair shining. But not the kind of angel that ever had anything to do with my life. "He likes me," she said. "I give him some attention once in a while."

It was like her to start in on me, even while seeming friendly. I slouched back against the bricks and looked at her through the hair hanging in my eyes. I looked like shit, and now I felt like shit—I didn't know how the Turners did this to me. She stepped up on the porch. "Do you mind if I sit down?"

"Hey, it's your porch." I moved aside the morning paper, and she sat down, tucking her short skirt underneath her tight little ass. She was sharp, no doubt about it. I sucked in my gut.

"Listen, I wanted to talk to you about the dog and everything. My husband and I don't want a feud." She lit a cigarette, then caught me staring at her. "Smoke?"

"Yeah, thanks." I squinted against the sun. The street was quiet. Bud sat at our feet—like a good dog, for once. "Sorry about last night. I was a little drunk. It's just that Bud...."

"My husband is sorry too. It's not easy being tactful at three in the morning."

I nodded my head. "You can say that again. What I want to know is if you're all hot for me to get rid of the dog, how come it seems like you like him?" I held Bud by the collar and patted his head. I knew she must have thought I was a real loser. I felt like I was waiting in some doctor's office and she was taking my medical history, a history I wasn't proud of.

"It's not that we don't like the dog. It's not his fault. Well, I don't mean to blame you. It's not anybody's fault, I guess. The main thing is he barks at night when you're not here."

"I know. I wish I could get on days—it'd be better if I was on days. Been working a lot of overtime, too. This boy needs to run a little more. While I'm going crazy at work, he's going crazy here." We sat smoking in silence, then she ground hers out hard into the cement, smashing it into shreds. I patted Bud on the belly, and he grunted.

"Yeah, I go out drinking now and then, too. Sometimes I get home pretty late."

"I know," she laughed. "I hear you stumbling up the steps some nights." She looked at her watch. "Listen, we just want you to know this is nothing personal. We hope you don't hold it against us. Maybe it's best for everyone, including the dog. I'll ask around," she gave me a teethy smile, "and see if I can find someone who'll take him."

Her voice rankled me some. I know when I'm being talked down to. "So, it's settled then, is it?"

She squinted at me. "What do you mean?"

"Well, it doesn't seem like I have much of a say in all this."

"Remember, we *asked* you to do something before."

"Yeah, yeah," I scratched Bud's chin. I wanted to say something clever, something that might put us back on the same level. I could smell her perfume and knew she could smell my sweat.

She touched my shoulder lightly. Like she was giving me a blessing. "I know it's hard. I had a dog once too." I shrugged off her hand—I almost wished I was talking to Turner instead. "And who are you, the Virgin Mary?"

She shook her head and laughed. "Not hardly. Come on, you'll find a place for him. Cheer up." She stuck out her hand.

I took it and held it for a second. "Okay, no hard feelings."

"Good. Fred will be happy. You know, despite the arguments, I think he does like you." She said that as if I should be honored. "I think you've got us—me—pegged wrong."

"We'll just be one big happy family," I mumbled as she turned away and started down the steps and on to the sidewalk. I stood up and looked down the street, saw Bud running toward her. It was too late—he jumped on her from behind, bouncing off the back of her legs. "Eddie!" she shouted, as if I was the dog. I called once, twice, three times, before Bud turned and ran to me. She shook her head, "Keep him on a leash—before he bites somebody." I grabbed Bud, led him in the house.

* * *

Before I went to work, I called the *Free Press* and placed an ad: "young springer spaniel, friendly, needs good home. Call 463-3495 btw. 11-2." My mother called to say she'd put an ad in the church paper too. I'm the oldest of five children, the only one not married, the only one who didn't leave town when the factory layoffs started and everything got tight around here. She reminded me my father's birthday was coming up. "At least get a card," she said. My father'd been a lifer too, at the same plant. He's retired now, and not much interested in what happens at work. I don't blame him. "You're not supposed to like your job, that's why they pay you," he told me when I came to him after my first week, ready to quit.

Maybe if I'd gotten an older dog who was already trained. But Bud was a six-week-old puppy when I picked him up last January at my uncle's farm out near Brighton. The last of the litter—part spaniel, part something else. I walked the last quarter mile because of drifts across the road. On the way home, holding him in my lap, I thought it would all work out. I was sure of it. He was the softest thing I'd ever touched. A year-and-a-half later, Bud still had too much puppy in him, too much energy to spend his days alone, chained in the yard.

When I started in at the plant right out of high school, I thought I'd only be there a few years, until I got enough money together to figure out what I really wanted to do. Eleven years later, I was still there. Maybe it was the new car that got me hooked, the payments I locked myself into during the years I might have been tempted to break away. I realized now how ugly it was compared to the original Mustangs. That's why I always have to say "Mustang *II*" — so people don't get disappointed when they see the car. Most people give a little laugh and shake their heads when they see it for the first time. What I wouldn't give to have one of the originals. Around Detroit, the rust gets everything in a few years. My brother Joe out in California tells me there are lots of old Mustangs still on the road out there.

I can't imagine a place where cars don't rust.

I washed my car every week, waxed it once a month for the first couple of years. Now, small pieces of rust fall off my driver's side door whenever I slam it. Though I could afford to go into debt again, I'm happy with my junker. Cars just don't have the attraction they did for me when I got that new one, though when I'm on the road sometimes I still find myself naming make, model and year of the cars around me, especially the older ones. In high school, me and my friends spent our time drinking beers and crawling under cars. My brothers used to look up to me then—they were always hanging around listening to us cuss and argue about who had the fastest car, about which girls we'd like to get into our back seats. I taught them all how to drive.

I rarely spent money on anything besides rent and my bar tab. I knew I was saving for something, but I wasn't sure what. I didn't want to buy a house—I was afraid of taking on more empty space. Besides, I knew I could always get laid off again.

* * *

At work that night, on my nine o'clock break, I tried to call Connie. At a phone booth near the front gate where it was quiet, I squinted at the smudged scrap of paper in front of me. It had spent the night in the back pocket of my work pants, and now it was blurred with sweat. I tried one number, but it was wrong. Tried another and got no answer. I kicked the booth, then went back to our break table which sat between two of the big presses. While I stared at the sheet of paper trying to figure out the number, I felt a punch in the shoulder. I turned around—it was BJ, my best friend in the plant. He pantomimed a smoking motion and nodded his head toward the factory yard. I shook my head. He shrugged and walked away.

I didn't know what it was, the thought of losing Bud or the talk with Lorraine Turner that afternoon, or fucking up the damn phone number, but I was really feeling desperate. Lorraine's smell and touch made me a little crazy. She was so beautiful and out of my league—I hated her. Kissing Connie in my car. Shit. Maybe she wasn't home. I could probably find her through Boomer's wife, but I wasn't sure I wanted to seem so hard-up to them. Boomer was one of my high school friends who'd done pretty well for himself. He went to school at Lawrence Tech and became an engineer. He worked for Ford's too—at the other end of things, as he liked to say. Who knows, maybe she gave me the wrong number in the first place.

In high school, I did pretty well for myself too, but I'm not exactly a prize now. Going bald, for one thing. Work kept me in pretty good shape. Had some muscles, though all the beer tended to gather around the middle. I ran out of breath trying to keep up with Bud on walks. In high school, I played football—one of the grunts on the line, just like now. I had few interests or hobbies outside work and the bar. Bud was one of those interests, but he'd be gone soon. I wondered if I'd been working in the factory too long—the crude, loud factory talk was what I was used to. I liked taking girls to the movies because then I didn't have to talk so much. I wondered what it'd be like to have a date with someone like Lorraine. What would we talk about?

The day after Boomer's wedding, I was pretty excited, thinking about Connie's laugh, the way she danced, her kiss. I hadn't had a girlfriend, a real girlfriend, since Cindy. Nine years since she dumped me. After graduation, she went away to college, and I started in the plant. I paid her a surprise visit around Halloween her freshman year. Her roommate tried to cover for her, calling "a friend's room" to tell Cindy I was there. I knew the story—what the guys in the plant had kidded me about since September was true—she'd gotten herself a college boy. As I stood waiting with her roommate, I planned how I'd kick the guy's ass. But Cindy took a long time to get there, and she was alone, and it was just real sad. I turned around and drove home. At work on Monday, a couple guys razzed me after word got out, but most simply patted me on the back or left me alone. Someone even suggested getting a carload to drive up and kick some college-boy butt.

I get maybe half-a-dozen dates a year. I know it probably seems weird, but I keep count. Working afternoons was a problem, and when things picked up at work, I put in a lot of overtime. When I do get a date, I can't seem to read the signals. I probably come across as seeming pretty horny—but, hell, I am. I'm comfortable in a place like the Ritz, but that's not a place to meet women unless you want to pay to get your rocks off in a van in the parking lot.

* * *

I sat in front of my locker, taking off my work clothes, wishing I'd smoked that joint with BJ. I thought of trying the number I'd gotten no answer at earlier, but it was late, and I was beat to hell. I scrubbed my hands with the cleansing powder that reminded me of sawdust; whatever it was, it scrubbed off the day's grease. Even when my hands were clean, I rubbed that stuff on them. It relaxed me, circling the water over my hands, trying to wash away another day—though it usually took a few beers across the street at the Ritz to really get clean of that place.

Bobbie Joe came up and washed next to me. BJ was a good old boy who never seemed to be bothered by what happened at work. He was always ready for a good time afterwards. Years ago, he tried to make it on his own as a carpenter, but lost too much money trying to establish himself. He packed it in for the security of the plant, and it was a secure job then—the boom years, as they called them now, when there were jobs for just about everyone. Bobbie Joe and his wife Caroline had me over for dinner once in a while, and Caroline sometimes helped find me dates. She was BJ's high school sweetheart, and they seemed happy together. Sometimes she'd come down to the Ritz and meet us for beers after our shift. She worked at K-Mart's world headquarters out in Troy. They were like an older brother and sister to me—at least that's what I'd tell them some nights around closing time. He worked in a different department at an easier job now, because of his seniority, but when I was hired in, me and BJ tossed axle housings onto pallets in department 16 together, one of the worst jobs in the plant. It was a shared job that either started fights or friendships. He carried more than his share until I got used to the hard work.

"BJ, you want a dog?"

"Hey, I've got enough trouble handling my old lady," he joked.

"I gotta get rid of my puppy—landlord says he goes or we both go."

"You should tell that landlord to cram it up his ass."

"I don't know if I want to fight it. I'm no fucking good for that dog. Either he's inside shitting on the floor or outside barking 'cause he's lonely. When I'm not working, I'm either at the bar or sleeping. I can't remember the last time I took him for a walk."

"I'm sorry, Eddie, we can't take your dog. Caroline and I decided a long time ago, no kids, no pets."

"I just can't take him to the pound. I've treated him shitty enough as it is. The least I can do is find him a good home."

"Okay, man, I'll spread the word. What about your folks?"

"My old man? With a dog? When we were kids, we had a dog that bit him on the ass. He took that dog straight to the pound. He said *kill this mother fucking dog.* It was the first time I heard my dad say *motherfucker.* I was ten, I think. I'd heard *shit* and *asshole* before, but never *motherfucker.*"

"Oh yeah? *Motherfucker* was my old man's nickname for me. He'd come home from work and say, 'How's my little motherfucker?' I can't remember if it started before or after my momma left us."

"Well, you're a *big* mother fucker now, BJ." I smiled and laughed, punching him in the shoulder, but I was remembering hating my dad for taking our dog away. Two of my brothers were a year apart, and so were my youngest brother and sister. I was three years older than any of them, the mistake that prompted the marriage. It was a worthless dog, but it was mine by default. Maybe I hadn't taken very good care of that dog either.

"This mother fucker's gonna beat your ass at the pool table tonight," BJ said.

I hesitated. "Nah, BJ, I'm beat. Heading home tonight."

BJ's jaw dropped, and he jumped back. "I can't believe it. Are you sick or something?" He shouted down the row of lockers, "Hey guys, Buford's not going to the Ritz tonight."

"Must be love," somebody piped in.

"Nah, I think Buford's too ugly for anybody to love."

"Maybe Buford thinks he's too good for us."

"Shit," I said, "Fuck you guys."

They locked up their lockers and quickly joined the wave heading out the factory gate. I hung back for a minute. It'd been a long time since I missed a night at the bar, but this Bud thing had me all twisted up inside. I punched myself in the side of the head. The humid August heat was suffocating me. I slammed the car door shut, threw my lunch bucket and thermos on the back seat. I started to squeal out of the parking lot, but had to slam on the brakes and get in line behind the others at the red light on Mound.

At home, I dug out the leash and took Bud for a walk around the block. He yanked me along, scrambling from tree to tree. It was after midnight—a few lights on here and there, but the streets were quiet. The Turners' apartment was dark. I didn't hear a thing as I climbed the stairs. I heard her moaning sometimes when they were going at it, but not tonight, and I was glad of it.

* * *

A week later, I still had Bud. Turner threatened me with an eviction order. I got some phone calls asking if he "had his papers" —if he was purebred. They'd hang up on me when I said no. "That's what's wrong with this country," I told BJ down at the Ritz, "everybody wants purebreds—nobody wants a dog just because it's friendly. Friendly don't count for shit anymore."

"Never did, bro, never did," BJ said, "But I'll buy you another beer anyway." We both laughed. It bothered me though. I started hanging up first, as soon as they asked the question. I didn't know quite sure why I got Bud, but it wasn't for his bloodline.

"Rich people are like purebreds—they inherit everything—like the Fords."

"And the GMs," BJ joked. "How come you don't hear about the GM family?"

"What a boring name for a company: General Motors. Would you drink a beer from the General Beers Co.?"

"If it tasted good, I wouldn't care if it was the Monkey Fart Beer Co." He let out a big belch. "Don't worry, somebody'll take that mutt of yours."

Everybody liked BJ. Our table at the Ritz was always busy, BJ handing out advice on everything from home improvements to taxes to marriage. He was a company man and never caused trouble. Even the foremen liked him. The monotony of the work never bothered him. "It's just like watching TV, man," he told me. "I just tune out."

* * *

I could by rights take every third weekend off if I wanted, but I hadn't taken one in six—weekends off had been pretty depressing, and I'd come to almost like the numbness of going in every day, the weeks blurring together. It scared me to think that I was one of the "old guys" now, one of the lifers, that my life outside work had come down to beer, TV, and a visit to my parents' once in awhile. I wondered if I'd ever be as content as BJ.

For a year, I'd shared a house with two other guys from work, and we had a lot of parties with not enough women and too much beer.

"The wrong crowd," my parents had said. "Where do I meet the right crowd?" I asked. One of the guys was married now, and the other moved to Texas. It didn't seem like much at the time, but I missed those guys—anything was better than the long quiet hours Bud couldn't quite fill.

At least a couple times a year, my mother asked me if I wanted to move back home, but I saw that as the final defeat. I knew my family and friends would snicker at that. I could imagine my brothers and sister coming home at Christmas and finding me back in my old room. Damn, that would kill me. And my mother already nagged me about my drinking as it was. And the old man, he'd have a field day. I had to do a lot of work breaking in my parents for the others. I spent too much time doing that and forgot to think about my own future. When my parents gave up and let me do what I wanted, I thought that meant drinking beer in the basement or staying out all night.

I never considered college. They placed me in the vocational training track in high school, and I stayed there like a good boy, trusting their judgment that I was dumb. I liked history, and I took a course once at the community college to make my mother happy. She believed they were wrong about me, about all her kids. They may have been wrong about a couple of us, but I don't know—maybe they were right about me.

My professor in the history course was a pale, skinny guy—bald, with a long beard. He told us he was a Marxist. I couldn't understand most of what he said. It seemed like he hardly ever talked about things that really happened in history, which is what I was interested in. Instead, it was all this theory and big words. I don't think anyone in our class knew what they meant. It was mostly housewives and a few guys like me who were still young enough to hope taking a few classes could change our lives. I got the prof out for a few beers after the last class and started arguing with the guy. He broke down and started crying right there in the bar, so I lied and told him he was a good teacher. It wasn't the Ritz—some fern place next to the school. I guess they don't make much teaching community college. We finally agreed it was all bullshit.

I had a fling with a married woman in the class, the wife of a salesman. When I think of that class, I think of her. She was bored and generous, and for a while it seemed like we loved each other.

It seems to me the more education a people have, the harder it is for anyone to understand what they're saying. It was that way with Turner too—when he started in with his legal mumbo-jumbo, I just scratched my head. "Now tell me that in English," I said when Turner came to me last. Turner said, "It means 'get rid of your dog'. Now."

"See this fist," I told him. "Know what this means?"

I probably sounded like what he expected me to sound like—a dumb-ass factory rat. Maybe I was trying to show him that he didn't scare me with his money and his status and his beautiful wife. But he did scare me. Threatening to punch him was the dumbest thing I could do. But what would've been a smart thing?

I decided that when my lease was up in a few months, I was leaving Turner's, dog or no dog.

* * *

Saturday morning, I sat on the porch, tired and surly after a long Friday night at the Ritz. I knew it was a weekend-long hangover I was dealing with—I could have just worked it off making double-time. I had Bud chained up out front. I couldn't worry about chasing him down this morning, and besides, I wanted him close by.

Around noon, Lorraine stepped out onto the porch in a white pantsuit that was almost see-through. I tried not to stare, but I couldn't help noticing the white of her bra and panties, the dark shape of her flesh. I groaned and squinted up into her face.

"Working today?" I asked.

"Yeah. Aren't you?"

"Nah. Taking a break. A couple old folks coming over later to look at Bud here." They'd seen my ad in the paper and had woken me up with a phone call that morning. They'd asked how well-behaved Bud was. "He's a prince," I lied through my haze. "Very calm." I'd been worried ever since.

"That's great!" Lorraine said.

"Yeah, I knew you'd be pleased...Hey, where's the old man?"

"He's up north visiting his mother."

I perked up a bit. "He left you here all by yourself? You probably need a break from him anyway. I'm not even married to him, and I need a break from him."

"Eddie," she said, one hand on her hip, her head cocked. But she smiled as if I'd hit a little truth. "Hey, where'd you get that scar?" She crouched down beside me and traced a thin scar running down my arm.

I was surprised again by her touch. "Piece of metal cut me, couple years back."

"How many stitches?"

"Fifteen."

"Whoever sewed it up was a butcher."

"Plant doctor. He's a drunk. No one bitches too much because you can bribe him to send you home on medical—and he's been known to dish out some choice drugs." I paused a moment. She was a nurse—it was worth a try. "Lorraine, I know we're not the best of friends, but you wouldn't happen to have something in your medicine chest to calm Bud down a bit when these people come to look at him?"

"Eddie, you've got to be kidding."

"No, I just want to mellow him out some. They want a calm dog. If he's doped up some, they might take him."

"Then after it wears off?"

"Then they'll like him so much they'll—"

"They'll be stuck with him," Lorraine said.

"No—put up with him. Like I do. Besides, he'll grow

out of this. Won't you Bud?" He turned from digging in the bushes and ran over, putting his paws on my chest and licking my face.

"How old are they? Think he'll grow out of it before they die?"

I closed my eyes. My head was burning up. "I don't know. All I know is the guy said he's retired. I tried to sweet-talk him some, but I'm not so good at that."

"I've noticed."

I swallowed. I needed a drink.

Lorraine stepped into the house. In a couple of minutes, she came back and dropped two pills into my hand. I didn't know what to say.

"Percs? Great. Lorraine, thanks."

"For my bad back."

"Yeah, I bet." I laughed. "One for me, one for the dog, right?"

"Don't get smart, or I'll take them back. One for now, and one for if you need to pull this scam again. It'd be a present for my husband if the dog's gone when he gets home."

"It'd be a present for me if your husband never came back," I mumbled. "Hey, you want me to pay you for these?"

She paused. "No—you owe me one."

"Listen, if I give up Bud, you'll owe *me* one. He's been great this last week or so."

"Amazing what a little attention will do. Look, I gotta go." She touched me on the shoulder. "Hope it works." She patted Bud hard on the head and walked away. I wasn't sure I wanted it to work.

I went in the house and crushed up part of the pill, then mixed it in with some ground-up bologna. Bud wolfed it down. I looked for signs as he circled the yard. His chain was long enough to let him cover a lot of ground, though I'd shortened it some to keep him out of Turner's flower garden. He said Bud howled during the night while I was at work. I didn't blame Bud—some nights driving home from work, I howled out the window myself. I watched him reach the end of the chain and get yanked back.

The old folks showed up around 3:30. I had cleaned up the crap in the yard and brushed Bud. I also shaved, showered, and combed my hair, put on clean jeans, and a sport shirt my mother gave me for my birthday.

"Hi," I said, smiling and sticking out my hand, wondering if I was being too cheerful, but they responded just as cheerfully. Bud was lying at my feet, stoned. He picked up his head and wagged his tail at them. They sat down, and Bud rubbed his head against the old man's leg. It was as if it'd been rehearsed. I gave them the dog's history and explained that a new landlord had bought the house who didn't allow pets. My hands shook as I tried to pet Bud. "Damn good dog," I said.

They bought it all, took Bud with them that afternoon, along with his chain, his bowl, leftover dog food—the works. I took a minute to say good-bye to him—hugged him hard, surprised myself by crying. I felt like Bud was the only thing worth holding onto in my life, and I was giving him away. Even as the tears came, I was angry with myself for getting sentimental. I closed my eyes, and the moment passed. I let go. As they got in the car, Bud climbed in behind them without hesitation.

Shocked by how quickly it had happened, I went out and bought a case of beer. I downed a couple quick ones, then fell asleep in the sun. When I woke up, it was almost dark. I called my mother and thanked her for her help. She was all sympathy and asked me to come over for dinner Sunday. I said yes, even though I knew after an hour, I'd feel claustrophobic there. It'd be a good first hour though, sitting in the old living room, staring at the TV, the old knickknacks and photos.

I tried the number in my pocket again—I couldn't remember which guess had gotten no answer before, but the number I tried this time was busy. "Fate," I said as I hung up the phone. I looked around: Bud's hair was everywhere. I tossed an empty beer against the wall, and it clunked to the rug near the door.

I boiled a couple of hot dogs for dinner while watching the end of a fight on TV. It was two heavyweights, and they hung on each other, hardly throwing any punches. I felt as exhausted and discouraged as they looked. I had to get out of the apartment, so I wolfed down the dogs and walked over to the closest bar — Angelo's pizza joint two blocks over. I never went to the Ritz on my days off — it reminded me too much of work, almost as if going to the bar was part of what I had to do to get paid. Besides, they'd only make fun of the way I was dressed. At Angelo's, I sat at a small table by myself and watched the families around me eat pizza and argue, the parents drinking pitchers of beer, and the kids drinking pitchers of Coke, everyone getting a little wired. I drank fast, drawing in the moist circles under my beer bottle on the checkered tablecloth. A banjo player came out and stood in front of the screen they used to show old movies on — and song lyrics. I'd forgotten about "Saturday Night Singalong." I paid the waitress, who reminded me what I was missing. "I'll sing along at home, okay?" She gave me a dirty look. Heading out the door, I heard the banjo player shout, "Everybody ready to sing?" As the door slammed shut, I heard muffled screams.

I wasn't sure I wanted to go home yet. I took the long way, through streets of barbecues and loud weekend voices. Like most neighborhoods around Detroit, mine was full of people who helped make cars. An old Mitch Ryder tune blasted from a passing car. It was like everyone felt they had to make as much noise as they could on their days off to convince themselves they were alive. Maybe that's why I'd worked so many weekends lately — I was tired of shouting.

* * *

Back home, I sat on the porch and opened another beer. I didn't want to climb the stairs again, so I walked into the yard and pissed under the tree. I missed the sound of Bud's jangling chain and started to get choked up again, standing there in the dark. I went back on the porch and caught my breath. Finally, I did go upstairs and sat at the kitchen table nursing the warm beer.

I heard the front door open, then Lorraine's voice shouting up the stairs. "Eddie? Eddie, are you up there?"

I walked out the door and leaned over the stairs. "They took him."

"Great!" she said. I closed my eyes and shook my head. "Or, not so great. Eddie, I didn't mean exactly...."

"I know."

"Listen...why don't we have a beer together? It's a nice night—we can sit on the porch."

"The neighbors might complain," I said sarcastically, but quickly added, "Sure." She was probably feeling sorry for me, or guilty. I didn't care—I was glad she asked.

"We'll whisper," she whispered.

I grabbed six long necks, sliding them between my fingers, and headed down the stairs.

"You don't mind if I'm a little sweaty, do you?" she asked.

"No problem. I drink with sweaty people all the time." I sat next to her on the stoop. It was a clear night. "Nice moon," I said.

She giggled. "Hey Eddie, you look pretty sharp tonight. You don't look half bad when you dress decent."

I tucked in my shirt. "Got dressed up for the visitors."

"How was Bud?"

"Fine. Cheers." I lifted my bottle. She clinked hers against mine and took a long swig. I watched her, then took a long swallow myself. She handled the bottle like she handled her cigarette—she knew what she was doing.

"Lorraine, I got a little something for you." I reached into my pocket and pulled out a handful of change and a couple of black capsules. I dropped the drugs onto her lap. I didn't know how she'd react, but drugs for drugs seemed like a fair exchange.

"Hey," she said, "what's this—speed? I don't do this stuff...anymore. I promised Fred."

I thought I'd screwed up again.

"But he's not here," she laughed and quickly popped one in her mouth. "Here." She gave me one back. "You take one too, and I'll tell you my life story."

"Cheers." I said again and tossed it in my mouth, took another swallow of beer. I was surprised as hell, almost a little giddy. We both put away two quick ones while she talked about herself. She went to Mercy College and was an RN, not a LPN—that distinction seemed important. She'd met Turner at a bar near the University of Detroit where he was in law school. His family was old money— Grosse Pointe money. Her family was from East Detroit, the working-class suburb that changed its name to eliminate the "Detroit" part because of its bad rep. It's called East Pointe now. She talked about her days in school like they were the best times in her life. I could relate to that.

"I can't tell you how good this tastes," she said, draining her bottle, setting it on the cement stoop. "I used to be pretty crazy, you know. In my younger days," she laughed. "Before I met Fred. When he finished school, he got a job with this big firm—his father's old firm. Ever since then, he seems so damn serious about everything. And he's always right, that's what kills me. He's really a nice man, though. He's been good to me. His family hates me."

"I used to be pretty crazy too."

"You're still pretty crazy, if you ask me. Sometimes when I hear you coming home drunk....I remember getting wasted, stoned, like in the old days. Listen—don't ever tell Fred this—I almost got married right after high school. To a guy something like you, a little rough around the edges—no offense." She looked down at the grass. I thought about the long, depressing nights at the Ritz and said nothing. I couldn't believe she was telling me this. I peeled the label off an empty bottle. I wanted to rest my hand on Bud's head to steady myself.

"We partied all the time," she said, "I guess I grew out of him once I started college. But sometimes I wish old Fred had a little more kick to him, if you know what I mean....Eddie, if you got out of the factory, I bet you could really go someplace. I almost didn't go to college. And I was thinking of quitting when I met Fred. He talked me into staying. I got a good job down at the hospital. Now look at me."

I looked. She talked on and on, about their dream house, the jacuzzi and sauna, the swimming pool. She brought out pictures. It turned out the reason she didn't go with Fred was that his mother wasn't speaking to her. And that she was pissed off at Fred because he didn't want her to see her old friends anymore.

"We'll have to have you out to the new house," she said.

I just shook my head at that one. "You must be stoned."

"Hey, maybe we can all go out sometime, me, you, Fred. He doesn't drink much, especially since we've been married. He thinks being married means you can't have fun anymore. If we get a couple in him, maybe he'll loosen up some."

"Ha," I said.

* * *

We finished the beers I'd brought down. She looked up at the sky and rubbed her arms.

"Cold?" I asked.

"Yeah."

"Maybe it's the speed." My heart blasted away in my chest. What the hell, I thought, and moved closer and put my arm around her.

"Hey," she complained, but she was smiling. "No funny stuff. I'm a married woman, you know." She laughed.

"Shit."

I laughed too. I didn't know she'd been busting to get out. "We've all got our chains, eh Lorraine?" I paused. "Why'd you marry him?"

"Oh, it was some stupid idea of growing up and being respectable. My parents love him. He's got money. But he's sucking up all my life," she blurted suddenly. "If he isn't, then something is."

"It sounds like you have your fun, judging from what I hear."

She shook her head, laughed, and swayed toward me. "You pervert."

"It's not like I *try* to hear or anything."

"Oh, Eddie," she said. She wrapped her arms around my neck and pulled me to her, kissing me awkwardly on the mouth, our teeth clicking. We wrapped our arms around each other and rolled off the steps and onto the grass. I ran my hands down her hips, over the tight uniform. "Wait. Eddie. Wait. Hold on." She froze, pushed me away. "We can't do this." I let go of her and sat back up on the stoop. She sat too. "Whew." She was breathing hard. "Eddie, you're a little wild. We can't get carried away here.

"Oh, shit, look what you did. I got grass stains on my uniform. How am I going to explain that to Fred? I'll have to get up early and wash these before he gets back. What time is it anyway?"

I held my head carefully between my hands, like it might break. It was throbbing. I couldn't believe the whole day. I was already trying to remember what Bud looked like, what her kiss was like. She got up and hurried past me into the house.

* * *

I knew it'd be awhile before the speed wore off. I started walking quickly, a speed walk—no sense of direction or purpose, just movement. I was pissed off at Lorraine and pissed off at myself. I wished Bud was there to pull me along, to give me some kind of focus.

I ended up along the edge of a city golf course, where I heard the sprinklers shooting off their timed spray. Floodlights lit the old clubhouse, a hangout for retired auto workers who played cards and golf for money. I jumped up and karate-kicked the air. I did it again, and again. I'd taken karate classes for a little while—when I was working midnights, I bought a lifetime membership in a club that folded within two years. I only went for about six months, then I got transferred back to afternoons, the deadly shift when all that was open after work was the bars. I was too tired after the factory to want to actually work out anyway. I thought it might be a way to meet or attract women. All it got me were some aches and pains. When I shifted to afternoons, I just couldn't make it there before going in to work. If only I'd get transferred to days. I kicked the air again.

The first green was partly lit by one of the floodlights. The flag stick was tilted, a beer can stuck on top. I stood waiting for one of the wings of spray to circle around to me. My skin tightened, but when the water hit, it only brought relief. Relief. The water gently slapped my face. I walked past and into the dark green of the fairways. I lingered at each sprinkler until, deep into the course, I was soaked skin through. I lay down on the soft grass of the 18th green and let the sprinklers circle their spray down over me. I wanted to take my clothes off, but I heard giggling nearby. A young man and woman were passing, holding hands. They laughed at me as if I was drunk or stoned. But I wasn't, not really. Here I was, both sober and not at work.

I'd saved a few bucks. My expenses were few. Maybe giving Bud away would actually free me up to change my life. My lease was up in a few months. Where would I go? What might I do? I knew there were no angels or saints, but sometimes I felt a certain magic in the world—I'd have a date with someone that would end with plans for another, I'd tell a story at work that everyone would laugh at, it'd feel good to visit my parents, and they wouldn't bug me. Maybe this would be the beginning of one of those times.

When I got back to the street, someone in a passing car yelled at me "Hey Vic," then something with "fuck" in it, then he held his thumb out in the air. I couldn't tell if it was a mean gesture or a friendly one, but I wasn't Vic, and that made me sad. I waved to the car in the distance.

On my way home, I passed an old man at a bus stop rocking back and forth on his heels, holding his lunch bucket in front of him like a pregnant belly. I passed a man staring at a mannequin in the window of a dress shop, mumbling a little prayer. I passed a punk kid in a dirty apron emptying garbage into a dumpster under the bright lights of a restaurant parking lot. I passed a crying woman in her robe sitting on the stoop of a house. My hands were shaking. I started walking faster. My clothes were already almost dry.

As I rounded a corner and headed back down my street, I noticed a dead squirrel in the road. Under the streetlight, I could see a little blood trickled from its open mouth. I know they tell you not to touch dead animals, but I pulled it to the side of the road. When I got back to the house, the first floor was dark. I stood for a moment in front of Turners' door. "What about my life story?" I shouted.

Jim Ray Daniels was born in Detroit and currently lives in Pittsburgh. He is the author of four books of poetry, including *Places/ Everyone, Punching Out, M-80,* and *Blessing the House.* He also edited the anthology *Letters to America: Contemporary American Poetry on Race.* His story "No Pets" was made into a feature film.

Bottom Dog Press
c/o Firelands College
Huron, Ohio 44839
Lsmithdog@aol.com